Every man has a peccadillo. Some are more peculiar than others. Can Kate cope with this one?

Kate meets her perfect man. He's rich, intelligent, handsome, and sexy. A genuine contender for the vacant post of husband.

But is there a catch? Is anybody really perfect?

Kate soon learns that her new man has some special needs. He's a submissive and loves to be spanked. In order to satisfy him, Kate needs to learn new skills, so she becomes an apprentice in the dungeon of a Dominatrix.

Will Kate find her inner Mistress? Has she got what it takes to dominate her man? Will the relationship survive?

The Dominatrix's Apprentice
Copyright © 2018 D.V. Roberts
ISBN: 978-1-4874-2059-8
Cover art by Martine Jardin

Published by eXtasy Books Inc or
Devine Destinies, an imprint of eXtasy Books Inc

Look for us online at:
www.eXtasybooks.com or www.devinedestinies.com

THE DOMINATRIX'S APPRENTICE
THE ADVENTURES OF A
HUSBAND HUNTER BOOK 4

BY

D.V. ROBERTS

The Dominatrix's Apprentice

"Hit me harder, my lord. Do not spare the rod," the near-naked woman demanded.

"You deserve it, my lady, you know you do," replied an imposing and authoritative male. "You did not obey my instructions, and you spent without permission."

As I heard the voices, I took in the scene in front of me and looked closely at the man. He was tall and fully dressed. The lady had addressed him as *my lord*.

Is he a real lord? He looks like one, or is this the lady just being respectful?

The *lord* was a very handsome young man with a mane of long brown hair. Was he wearing a wig or was this his own hair? He was dressed in a crisp white shirt, silk waistcoat, blue coat with brass buttons, dark-coloured breeches, white stockings, and black buckled shoes. The shoes were polished to a high sheen and reflected the multitude of candles which, in the absence of electric lamps, were the sole source of illumination for the room in which the three of us stood.

Very late eighteenth century. Very Regency.

He was a fine specimen of a gentleman and held himself with pride and dignity, much as some favoured dandy would have done in the royal inner circle of those turbulent times. I looked at his trousers and noticed the bulge there at the front, straining to burst the shiny buttons, which were all that held back his engorgement. It was obvious that he was sexually aroused and enjoying himself spanking the woman.

The *lord* was standing in the middle of the candlelit room with a wooden paddle in his right hand. My attention switched to the woman. She had a mane of wonderfully pleated hair cascading over her bare arms, with delicate fresh flowers embedded in her magnificent coiffure. Her only garments were white stockings and a black garter belt. I could see her delicate, slender form with supple breasts but could not see her face. Her arms were stretched upwards, and she was tied by her wrists to a rope hanging from the ceiling.

I took in my surroundings of red painted walls and a deep soft Turkish carpet under my feet. There was a candelabra in each corner. The room was very sparsely furnished. I noticed a bed, a bench, and an ottoman. There were other items of furniture, too, but their shapes were peculiar and unfamiliar, and their purpose was unknown to me.

He hit her again. This time the stroke of the paddle was much harder, and he grunted with the effort, his long hair flying up and then falling back on his shoulders. The paddle landed straight on the pink cheeks of the lady's naked bottom, emitting a pleasant *smack* sound as it did.

The woman squealed in appreciation.

"That's good," she gasped. "I want more of it. Please punish me, my lord, as I did wrong you. I did not obey your instructions, I spent without your permission, and I deserve to be punished by you."

She was obviously enjoying being hit by a paddle on her exposed bare bottom, which had now changed its colour to a crimson red...

The gentleman was delighted with her response.

"You are a mean, disobeying harlot," he shouted, swinging the paddle back for an even harder strike. He then swung his arm forward and whacked the young woman's buttocks again.

She squealed once more. "Yes, my lord, I am a mean, disobeying harlot. I deserve my punishment. There is no excuse for spending without your permission."

What has she spent? His money? What's going on here? Why

am I standing in a room watching a Regency-era gentleman administering this punishment and for what reason? Why is her crime of spending without permission so great? What does it really mean?

Is she a shopaholic maidservant and he a controlling master punishing her for overspending?

"You've displeased me," shouted the lord, "you need to control yourself more, you can only spend when given permission."

He put the paddle away on a chair nearby and took from there another tool of torture, something which looked like a leather whip with many endings. I suddenly realised what it was. This was the famous cat-o'-nine-tails. I'd seen a picture of it some time ago and was appalled that it was still used in some countries to administer corporal punishment.

And it was definitely in use in the Royal Navy during that period.

Surely he is not going to hit her with this. It would be appalling. Why would a gentleman like him want to punish this young woman so severely? What was her great crime that she ended up deserving such harsh punishment?

He came close to his victim and started fondling her buttocks with his right hand. He then slid his hand between her thighs, touching her feminine treasures and feeling her dampness.

Oddly, the expression on his face was one of stern disapproval.

"You are already well aroused," he said, apparently displeased.

"Yes, Master, I am sorry, my lord."

"This is without my permission."

"I am very, very, sorry, my lord, please forgive me again."

This time the man said nothing while eyeing her magnificent behind. And so the woman continued to speak, her voice quiet and submissive, yet somehow filled with desire and frustration.

"Oh, my lord," she said. "I am so weak. I have no control over my body—as soon as you touch my altar of love, I am ready to spend. Please have mercy on me."

He looked sternly at her, while vigorously rubbing his erection with his right hand, which he had withdrawn from the lady's pink buttocks.

"You need to control your body better," he remarked, an injunction that patently he did not apply to himself. He removed the fingers of his left hand from her intimate area and stood back. He brought those same fingers, wet from the lady's juices, to his lips and licked them, savouring her, while masturbating himself even harder.

"You are such a harlot," he said with contempt. "You are already very wet between your legs—you have no control whatsoever."

Then with both hands, he started manipulating the top of his trousers, undoing the buttons. He worked fast, his hands trembling with excitement. With the last brass button opened, his magnificent cock was free, released at last from its torment, poking proud and unashamed out of his breeches, all red and glistening in its glory. The man stroked himself and seemed to be very pleased, seeing his manhood in such great form.

This bizarre scene developing in front of me was fascinating. It was like I was watching a film, yet I was part of it, standing in this peculiar room and observing the couple. I didn't feel out of place, and for some bizarre reason I felt I was integral to the drama.

It struck me that this was all very duplicitous behaviour from the gentleman—if I could call him that at all. He was obviously a man of high standing in Society. I knew that this was so from his confident bearing and arrogant behaviour. Yet whacking a near-naked woman while berating her for being sexually aroused was not very gentlemanly behaviour, was it? So he could get excited and aroused in this situation, yet he forbade such arousal to his young victim. Disgraceful. I saw this young woman as a victim involved for whatever reason in this wicked game.

Somehow, though, they had not seen me, and somehow, I could not rouse myself to interrupt these depraved proceedings.

So all I could do was stand my ground and wait, with fascination, for the situation to develop further.

The man then put the whip into his right hand and approached the young woman from behind. He cracked the cat-o'-nine-tails on the floor, to let the woman know that her punishment for *spending* without his approval was to be harsh indeed.

He raised his hand, preparing to whack her with the whip, but in the middle of the movement, he suddenly changed his mind. His hand dropped, and he put the strings of the whip on her bottom and moved them gently up and down her central crack.

The woman wiggled her behind and squealed with pleasure.

"Oh, my lord," she gasped, "that's so tickly. I love it. Thank you, oh, thank you."

Then the lord withdrew the whip and without a word pressed his cock towards the opening of her bottom. I watched his bare, hairy buttocks move up and down as he rubbed himself on the woman's still-red behind, his breeches down at his ankles, covering the shiny black shoes.

Is he going to play with her buttocks only or is he going to penetrate her?

I watched in fascination and, to my horror, felt that I was also aroused myself. I was disgusted that my body could have such a reaction to the situation developing in front of my eyes. I'd never been into the hitting-and-punishing-your-lover stuff during sexual encounters, yet I could not help my body responding to the violent but sexy scene in front of me.

Or was the stimulant responsible for my arousal, specifically the view of the gentleman's naked, hardened cock, exposed in its full glory? I could see the vein throbbing along his penis and the foreskin pulled down exposing the head. Yes, without doubt this was a magnificent specimen.

It seemed that the young woman was also very impressed with the feel of his hard cock on her bottom.

"Oh, my lord, you are quite ready. Please let me suck you?"

The lord carried on rubbing himself on the opening to her anus, while seizing her breasts and suddenly planting a hard kiss on her lips, as her head turned towards him.

Then he stepped back, his dick wiggling as it detached from her evidently slightly sticky bottom.

"You want to taste my cock—you want to be a cock-sucker?" he rasped.

"Yes, Master, I do, it would please me a lot. I want you to spend in my mouth, and I want the honour of swallowing your heavenly juices."

The lord seemed to consider this request for a moment. It was almost as if he were being tempted into leniency, but then he roused himself back to strictness and shouted, "No. Not yet, not now, you still need to be punished for your disobedience."

And with those words, he stepped back and hit the young woman on her back with the cat-o'-nine-tails.

She screamed with pain, arching her spine and head backwards. After a couple of seconds, she then spoke. "Thank you, Master. Please, can I have some more?"

She wants more beating? She must be mad...

The next whack landed on her buttocks, and I could see red lines on her bottom cheeks where the strings of the whip had struck her.

The lord kneeled and undid the garters. He started removing the stockings, each of his hands working down one leg.

"Oh, my lord," said the woman, "your touch is so exciting, so gentle, yet I know your hands are so strong, so manly, so powerful." Despite being viciously beaten, the lady actually seemed appreciative of what he was doing.

He took the stockings and the garter belts completely off, and she gracefully stepped out of them. He picked them up and threw them away.

Now the man moved to her front. Maybe her face had a momentary flicker of defiance because the expression on his face seemed to darken. He grabbed her by her hair and pulled it towards him. She did not expect such an assault and moaned softly.

"Oh, my lord," she said, "please kiss me again and take me. Take me right now, right here. My secret garden awaits you in all your glory, and I am ready to spend again. May I have your permission?"

"Permission denied." The man's voice was full of anger now.

Is he pretending to be angry? Or is his fury real?

"You have disobeyed me previously," he spat. "For now, I will punish you again, so you remember never to spend without my permission."

Spending again. Finally, I got it. The words spend, spending, or spent were a substitute for orgasm. So this poor lady had had an orgasm without the *lord's* permission, and for this he was punishing her. Severely.

What a jerk this bastard lord must be. And why has this young woman allowed herself to be put in such a position and to be at the mercy of such a beast? How come she is able to enjoy pain and have orgasms while being hit by a whip?

Yet the sight of his extended stiff penis brought more heaviness into my belly. I wouldn't mind sampling it myself, obviously without the flogging. Should I step in and touch his cock? Would they welcome me into their scenery? Would she be happy with another lady stealing the favours of his magnificent manhood?

I still could not see her face. I was afraid to move, as I didn't want them to notice that I was watching them, not yet. I was not sure if either of them was aware of my presence, although their lack of acknowledgement of me suggested that I was somehow invisible to both of them.

I did not want to infuriate the man by appearing unless I could be sure that my presence would be welcome. He might have some ideas about putting me in the same situation as his current victim and punishing me with a whip for my perceived failures.

I saw him take the whip into his right hand again. His expression softened, and while still holding the lady's head, he stroked her belly and her breasts with the strings of the cat-o'-nine-tails.

Her body quivered. She said, "Oh, my lord, please, may I?"

The man gave her a sinister smile. "Be patient," he replied, "and your patience shall be rewarded."

The woman was obviously disappointed by this answer.

"Oh, my lord, my Master, I beg of you, please let me spend..."

He became angry. "No, I said no. Don't you understand, you wicked harlot? No means no."

He let her head go and stepped away while raising his right hand. He brought it down, and the cat-o'-nine-tails hit the woman on her breasts. She cried out.

"Oh, my lord, please forgive me for asking."

I'd had enough watching this nasty stuff. He hit her on her breasts, and she screamed. Now I was totally appalled. This was awful and must have been terribly painful for the lady. Breasts should be honoured, kissed and admired, not whacked by a whip.

What sort of monster would behave this way?

I wanted to rip the whip out of the lord's hand and use it to hit him with all my strength, straight on his swollen, sticking-out cock. Then he would know how painful it was when someone hit your breasts.

I wanted to shout at this man. How could he abuse this young lady so much with this twisted game? I wanted to tell him to stop, to tell him that he should let her go, and I wanted to go towards the young woman and comfort her and tell her that such humiliation and subjugation was not on, now we're in the twenty-first century. Times had changed.

She should never, ever allow a man to treat her like this, strip her naked, and beat her up.

So, feeling utterly enraged, I stepped forward, shouting at the man.

"Hey, your lordship, bugger off and leave her alone, you depraved pervert. How dare you beat up a woman for your twisted, kinky perversions? How dare you?"

The lord took no notice of me. It was as if I wasn't there — he completely ignored my shouting.

By contrast, the young woman seemed to notice my attempt at defending her. She turned her face and looked straight at me, trying to say something.

Then I saw her face, and the shock of seeing it stopped me in my tracks. I recognised her face. Despite everything I'd just witnessed, I knew her. *It's me — my face — staring out of a mirror.* It was as if she were the identical twin sister I'd never had. She was either me in some distorted reality back in the eighteenth century, or a doppelganger.

Suddenly, she spoke. I could hear her voice. It was just like my own voice. She was speaking directly to me.

"Kate, please stop this."

Stop what? I didn't understand what she was asking of

me. To put a stop to this situation or to stop shouting at the man? I was totally confused, the likeness of the lady to me was so very unsettling.

I decided that she wanted me to stop the situation and help her. I prepared myself to take the man on. He was much taller than me, but if I freed the woman from her ropes there would be two of us against him. We could overpower him and put a stop to this young lady's suffering.

I also realised that she'd called me Kate.

How does she know my name? Who is she anyway? My long-lost identical twin?

Suddenly I heard another sound. Classical music. The tune of *Ode to Joy* from Beethoven's ninth symphony was playing in this strange room.

* * * *

I blinked, and when, a moment later, my eyes opened, I found that I wasn't standing up at all, and the woman, who looked like me, and the man, had both disappeared. The strangely lit and oddly furnished room had also vanished.

And I was lying in my bed, in my lovely new home. It was all a dream. Albeit a very vivid, very realistic dream, in glorious Technicolour. One of several weird dreams I'd experienced lately. The music, though, was real enough. It was coming from the alarm clock set up to a classical music channel.

I'd decided earlier this week that listening to the voice of the prime minister waking me up in the mornings had got a bit too much. So I'd changed stations on my radio alarm clock to Classic FM.

Why was the man beating the woman and enjoying it so much? Why was the scene taken from the late eighteenth century?

Why did the young woman in the dream look exactly like

me? Was it me in my past life or a doppelganger? If she was a stranger, how come she knew my name?

Well, it was quite a dream. It brought shivers to my body now when I thought about it being fully awake.

I will never, ever allow a man to beat me up.

So why was my identical twin allowing it? Was she really enjoying it? Strange...

I suddenly realised that my dream reflected the book I'd finished reading last night—a dark story about love, lust, and sadomasochism. The action was set in the eighteenth century, and the characters spoke in an archaic, aristocratic manner. This was not a story of a lord—not even a pretend one—and his woman. This was a story of an aristocratic married couple enjoying this sort of relationship. And, yes, he was calling her names, too.

Somehow my subconscious mind had taken that story and turned it into a tale of personal victimisation by a Regency dandy.

Oh well, I've never been in such a situation myself in real life, and I never will be.

I didn't think I would ever enjoy it. Not for me, then. I wouldn't want to be whacked while standing naked. Being dressed wouldn't make it any better.

But then a thought occurred to me. Would I be able to whack another person if the roles were reversed?

The answer entered my head as quickly as the question was posed.

Only if I hated him enough.

I got into the shower and turned on the water to its preset temperature. A jet of hot water came out, striking me on my chest. *Lovely.* Then my thoughts turned to the challenges of the day ahead at work, and the memory of last night's dream faded as I concentrated on the tasks ahead of me.

* * * *

"Were you the submissive or the Dominant?" said my gloriously handsome gay assistant, Andy, at the office. He was pacing up and down the richly carpeted floor of the office of the Head of Marketing for our group of colleges—that would be me. He was very intrigued by the short summary I'd given him of *The Adventure of The Lord and the Naked Woman*, but he'd got the wrong end of the stick.

I shook my head but didn't rise from my lovely leather chair, a far cry from the stool I'd had as the lowly head of accounting just a few months previously.

"Neither, Andy," I said. "It's like I said, in my dream I was just an observer watching a Regency-era gentleman spanking a naked woman with a paddle, then later hitting her with a whip. This was supposed to have been a punishment for her having her orgasm without his permission."

Should I have mentioned to Andy the woman's facial similarities to me? No, that bit's all much too weird.

Andy stopped pacing and looked at me. "Seriously?" he said. "Punished for having an orgasm?" He giggled. "Frankly, I have no experience of the female orgasm myself, but friends of mine tell me that it doesn't interfere with a man's pleasure. So why would this lord want to do this?"

I felt irritated. We had work to do, and I hadn't intended this extra-curricular chat to go on for so long. "I dunno, Andy, I really don't. Anyway, back to the sales figures, please."

But Andy was not to be put off so easily.

"Well," he said. "Sounds like a dream about a man controlling a woman. Good thing you were just an observer and not a participant, or that would demonstrate all sorts of stuff..."

Gosh, he's getting a bit too close to the implications of the Naked Woman being my doppelganger...

Andy went back to his desk and seemed ready to focus on the business of the day. Then suddenly, he was back on the topic of dreams.

"You see, Kate," he said, a bit pompously, "I know quite a bit about the psychology of dreams. They are your brain's method for filing and filtering memories, feelings, and desires." He giggled again. "Are you into sadomasochism, Kate? Or would you like to be? There's no shame, you know. All sorts of perfectly respectable people enjoy this sort of kinky stuff."

I sighed and closed my laptop. It seemed that work would have to take a back seat for the moment.

"No, Andy," I said. "I'm definitely not into sadomasochism. I just happened to read a book about it yesterday and, to pick up on your concept, I think this was my brain's method of filing it in a hidden cabinet. I have no wish to open that cabinet ever again. So let's get back to doing what we're paid to do, shall we?"

I didn't think I really enjoyed the book about the S and M couple from the eighteenth century. I'd got it from Amazon on my Kindle and read it on the train while coming back from a meeting in Glasgow. The book was number two in the Amazon erotica section, so I had thought it might be good. *Wrong.*

I couldn't face up to the fact that the book, irrespective of its lack of literary qualities, had touched something dark and deep in my subconscious.

Andy was irrepressible. Once we'd drilled our way through some very good sales figures, he returned to the subject of the day.

"Well, Kate," he said. "It sounds like you had quite a vivid dream. Only one way to resolve all those hidden issues. You need to get laid, girl. When was the last time Luciano attended to your needs?"

Luciano was my awesome Italian Stallion, who assiduously, if insufficiently frequently, gave me my required internal massages. "Two weeks ago," I replied, giving Andy a truthful answer, which I shouldn't have done. *Damn.*

"Anyway," I continued, "this is none of your business, and remember I am your boss."

"Yes, my lady," Andy responded, giving me a mock bow. "Thank you for sharing your dream experience with your obedient servant." He leaned back in his chair, chewing a pencil with a pensive air. "You know, Kate, I, your obedient and humble servant" — another mock bow — "am not into S and M myself, but I do know someone who is."

I was getting ready to nip into the boss's office to show him how my appointment as Head of Marketing had transformed our sales performance and therefore swelled his personal bank account. Nevertheless, I was intrigued by Andy's comment.

"Hmm, interesting," I said. "Is your friend gay?"

"No," said Andy, "he's straight, but that's frankly irrelevant. You can be into S and M irrespective of gay or straight."

The memory of the lord's revolting behaviour from my dream made me resent this unknown man.

"What a disgusting creature he must be," I said, "whipping a woman in order to get his sexual needs fulfilled."

But Andy had news for me. "Ah, you're wrong about that, Kate," replied my in-house expert on sexuality. "This man's actually a submissive."

I was intrigued again. "A submissive?" I said. "So he needs to find a woman to beat him up to get his kicks? How strange..."

"Well, Kate," responded Andy, in the manner of a sophisticate delivering some worldly wisdom to his naive mouse of a boss. "I've heard that sadomasochistic behaviour is actually more about control on the Dominant's part and having no control and being humiliated on the other person's part than anything really about sex." He paused. "However, I only know a limited amount. It's not my kind of scene."

I was going to ask Andy what his scene was when the phone on my desk rang. It was the boss summoning me to his office.

"Much as I would love to hear more about your deep psycho-sexual knowledge, Andy," I said, picking up the papers with the sales figures, "our esteemed lord and master has called me into his office. He takes priority over my education on sadomasochism."

Andy winked at me as I left and said, smiling, "Go for the boss, Kate, don't be shy, girl. He's a much better bet than the lord from your dream, you know."

Andy was constantly encouraging me to get it on with our big boss.

"Oh, shut up, Andy," I said quietly, as by then I was already in the corridor walking towards the boss's office.

* * * *

"Good morning, boss," I said brightly as I came into his office. "I've got the monthly sales numbers for you." I put the sheet on his mahogany desk with a triumphant air, almost flamboyantly. "Revenues for last month double the previous."

I'd always had this feeling that the boss was, in some ways, an uncomplicated person. Money in his pocket, good. Money not in his pocket, bad. He could be generous and did not stint on staff parties and the like, but you always needed his approval to spend company cash. The trick was to persuade him that the expenditure was temporary and would produce a return to him personally in short order.

Understanding these basic principles lay at the heart of the Marketing Director's job. I understood them. My predecessor, Cameron, fired for the heinous sin of not generating enough revenues, and for the lesser sin of pot-smoking in the office, had not understood them.

The boss reviewed the numbers for a few moments and then his countenance lightened. "Splendid, Kate," he said. "I knew my judgement about you was correct."

He stood and marched around the desk, forcing me to twist my neck to see him.

"I didn't get where I am today," he continued, "without knowing that you would be the right person to replace that Cameron. You see, Kate, I'm a great judge of character and of ability, and you definitely have both of these qualities in abundance."

He paused, inviting a reply.

"Yes, boss," I said. In the circumstances, what else could I say?

"Now then, Kate," continued the boss, returning to his seat. "Topic of the hour. Nay, topic of the century!" He threw his arms up and then leaned forward towards me, his elbows on the desk, his head resting on his fists, and a look of intense focus in his eyes.

He was obviously about to deliver himself of a thought of great profundity. So I tried to appear excited, intrigued and awed, all at the same time.

"Emerging markets, Kate," said the boss. "Russia, China, India, Brazil, Korea. Those sorts of places." He leaned back in his chair, evidently pleased with himself.

"Yes, boss," I said, "you're quite right. We should definitely be targeting more students from those markets."

I was about to enlarge on this, pointing out that our penetration of those areas of the world was inferior to the achievements of another college group, run by the boss's friend and arch-rival, Stephen Smith, with whom the boss played an extremely aggressive game of competitive squash every week, when I realised the boss had more to say himself. So I shut up.

"Kate," he said, his gaze boring into me, "you're a fluent Russian speaker, so I know you can be relied on personally to progress things in that part of the world. But what about China? Huge market, millions of people, all wanting to come here to our college group, learn things and pay fees."

At least he prioritised the learning over the paying.

"So I want to increase your human resources in the marketing department," continued the boss, in the manner of someone about to bestow a great favour on me. "I'm transferring Daiyu Chen into your team. She's from Hong Kong, really energetic, keen as mustard to get us lots of Chinese students, and a big admirer of you, I might add. Oh, and fluent in Chinese." He threw himself back into his chair. Clearly pleased with himself.

"Mandarin," I said.

The boss looked a bit flummoxed at my remark.

"What's oranges got to do with this?" he said.

"No, boss," I said. "Not mandarin oranges, the fruit. Mandarin, the language. The principal language of China. They speak Cantonese mainly in Hong Kong. Quite different. I'm just wondering if Daiyu speaks both."

The boss looked slightly irritated at this. "Well," he said, "she's bound to speak all relevant dialects. Clever girl. So we're agreed, aren't we? You'll take her on and get me lots of lovely students who speak Chinese and are eager to learn English."

He picked up the telephone and started to bark orders at his PA. Our meeting was over.

As I stood to go, the boss put his hand over the phone's mouthpiece and said to me, "That will be all for now, Kate. You're doing great. I'm pleased I appointed you as the Head of Marketing. My intuition did not fail me. In fact, it never does."

"Yes, boss, great idea," I said. "I will definitely talk to Daiyu and involve her in marketing for the Chinese market. Anything else?"

I looked at him, and he opened his mouth. He stared back at me and, to my surprise, reddened slightly, as if he was trying to work himself up to saying something more.

No words came out. At that moment, his PA came in to the office. The boss closed his lips, pursing them, shook his head, and said distractedly, "No, Kate, thanks, that'll be all for now."

"Thank you, boss," was all I was able to respond to this. I left his office and closed the door behind me.

Whatever else he was really going to say to me, I wasn't going to hear it.

As I walked back to my own office, a vision of a very pretty mini-skirted twenty-something Chinese girl came to mind. The aforesaid Daiyu Chen, whom I'd met several times, and who'd been working in the secretarial team for the last three months. She was definitely highly intelligent and very motivated, having frequently pressed me for a role in the marketing team. Clearly, my lack of immediate enthusiasm had led her to cut me out of the loop and go straight to the top, to the boss. And that had worked.

Suddenly I felt a pang of jealousy. Did the boss fancy her? She certainly had legs all the way up to her bottom, as the phrase goes, and made good use of them. Or maybe this was the boss being wholly professional, trying to use his workforce efficiently. And I couldn't doubt the sense of involving her. From my point of view, a junior Chinese reporting to me was much less of a career threat than someone older.

Then it hit me. *Is the boss thinking of replacing me as Head of Marketing with Daiyu Chen? Am I going to train my future replacement?*

"Oh, stop being paranoid, Kate," I told myself sternly. "She's just a girl who happens to be bilingual, and we need a

Chinese speaker to help with Chinese students. All very sensible on the boss's part. Really."

But I still felt jealous, even if the professional worry seemed unnecessary. I had this vision of Daiyu sitting on the boss's desk, mesmerising him with her long bare legs swinging in front of his eyes, while she giggled at his jokes.

Why am I feeling jealous about the boss? I don't fancy him, surely?

The boss seems to have lost some weight. He looks really handsome, dressed in his dark-navy suit.

No, the boss is off limits.

Getting involved with him would ruin my career.

And I suddenly remembered the failure of my so-called relationship with Patrick, the English language teacher in one of our colleges. The recollection made me shiver. That had been a disaster. No, I must learn the lesson that whole Patrick thing had taught me. The workplace is not a good source for any sort of intimate relationship.

Anyway, tomorrow I had a first date with a great-sounding young man called Hugh. Recalling that with satisfaction, I marched back into my office to tell Andy about Daiyu joining the team.

* * * *

My date with Hugh was on Friday afternoon after work in a West London cafe. My date and potential husband candidate was a successful banker working for a major international bank with offices in the City and Canary Wharf, thirty-four years old, and single. We'd had several pleasant chats over the phone and had started flirting already. He seemed to have a nice sense of humour and told me that he was looking for a life partner and marriage.

So far so good. I hoped that, at a face-to-face meeting, we would get on just as well.

I'd responded to his advert in the Kindred Spirits Telegraph section, and we'd already exchanged photos. He seemed to be a good-looking guy, brown eyes, dark-blond hair, and a nice smile. He was three inches taller than me, so there'd be no problem with me wearing high-heeled shoes. I was very excited, preparing to meet my new potential life partner—all the signs for a good relationship were there.

He'd already called me several times after he'd got my photos and was gushing about my *beautiful maiden looks*. I wasn't sure what he meant by the *maiden* part—as a synonym for *virgin*, it was scarcely apposite to me, but hey, so far so good.

I supposed he was just using some archaic style of language. That's okay, all part of the dating game.

I took great care preparing for the date, dressing up in some of the expensive new clothes I'd bought with the enhanced salary that had come with my promotion at work. I put on some new sexy lingerie. I loved the feel of the silk encasing my bottom and admired my new bra pushing my breasts up and making them appear much bigger than they really were. I took out a beautiful little black dress, clear sheer tights, and a new pair of Steve Madden silver-coloured high-heeled boots. I'd discovered the Steve Madden brand of shoes only recently. I'd fallen in love with them and had bought two pairs. There were so comfortable, well worth the money I'd paid for them. *Really, they were.* Anyway, I was worth it—I kept repeating the slogan to myself.

I then did my makeup, and hey presto, a sexy Kate emerged from the super-efficient business Kate of earlier in the day. I was ready to conquer the new man. Whether he would turn out to be the man from my sexy dreams—my dream lover—I could not yet know, but I knew we were going to have a fabulous time.

I picked up my Givenchy handbag and my coat and was ready to meet the new man in my life. I decided to call an Uber taxi.

I'd obviously done a great job with my clothes and coiffure, because the Uber driver ogled me a bit—no, more than just a bit, he positively leered at me—but he said nothing. I gave him the address of my destination, and the conversation during the short journey was mainly about the English weather.

The café I'd stipulated for the date was in Chiswick. This was not that far away from Acton where I now lived, and Chiswick was a nice and upcoming area full of little shops and cafés.

I entered the café and recognised him straight away. He was even more handsome in real life than in his picture. He was sitting in a corner dressed in a dark suit—his cashmere coat put over another seat. A bunch of flowers was lying on another spare seat. I noticed a young waitress who'd brought him a cup of coffee. She seemed to be attracted to him and spent more time than strictly necessary over-energetically arranging the cream jug and the sugar bowl.

As I approached his table, the waitress had a quick look at me and immediately disappeared from sight.

Bugger off. This is my man, not yours.

My date got up from his chair as I walked up, and we shook hands, introducing ourselves formally, and he gave me the bunch of flowers.

Quite unusual, though, he's a gentleman, thoughtful and respectful. This feels like a good omen for the relationship.

So I sweetly thanked him and admired the flowers.

"Oh, Hugh," I gushed, "these flowers are wonderful and smell so nice. I really love red roses—red is my colour, how did you know?"

"Well," said my handsome date, tossing his blond hair in

a very fetching manner, "lovely flowers for a *very* lovely lady. I thought that red roses would go very well with your
inner and outer beauty."

His voice was rich and deep. *And he smells good, too. A fine
start.*

Pleasantries out of the way, we started chatting. I wanted
to know as much as possible about my companion. *Better to
find out any issues sooner than later.*

"So, Hugh," I said, getting straight down to it, "you are
good-looking, charming, and obviously in a good job. Why
are you still single?"

He seemed shy, almost embarrassed by the directness of
my question. I hoped I didn't sound too much like an inter-
viewer on *The Apprentice*.

"Well," he said slowly, "I was married before, but the
marriage was quite short. When we met we both lived in
London, but she wanted to move out, and we bought a
house in Esher." He took a sip of his coffee and paused as
the young waitress appeared again to take my order. She
seemed to be behaving professionally now and had stopped
looking at Hugh.

Kate One, Young Pretty Waitresses Nil. I may be a feminist,
but it was bitch-eat-bitch sometimes out there, and I was in a
combative mood tonight.

"Coffee for me, too, please, cappuccino with no sugar," I
ordered, and the waitress left promptly without a glance at
Hugh.

"So, Hugh," I continued, trying to make my tone a little
less inquisitorial, "you bought a house in posh Esher." I
knew the houses were posh as I'd been there once to visit a
friend. "And she was not happy with it?"

"Well," continued my handsome admirer, "she was happy to start with but became less happy with my long hours
at work. I had to get up quite early to come to the bank and
be at my desk when the markets opened—I'm a commodi-

ties trader, by the way, and sometimes it takes me as long as three hours to get back home. The traffic in London can be horrendous."

"Couldn't you have travelled by train?" I asked. "Surely the trains into Esher are quite good for commuting to the city."

"That's how I started," replied Hugh, "but my car had been vandalised in the train station car park, and I decided that coming all the way in by car was a better option. We have a secure car park at work, and I love driving. My car is like my second home. I can listen to music and make some phone calls when stuck in the traffic. It would be impossible to discuss financial transactions when stuck on the train."

Well, this seems a reasonable explanation. Some men do treat their cars as a member of their own family and can get quite attached.

"Do you have children together, I mean, with your former wife?" *Obviously not with his car, silly me.*

"No," said Hugh, sipping his coffee, "we don't. Divorce is much easier if you have no children. With hindsight, you know, I don't think I trusted her enough for that," he mused. "Starting a family is a huge responsibility, and you have to make sure that the woman you choose to be the mother of your children is a good one."

"But you married her," I said, a bit insistently, "so you must have loved her to start with, and I suppose she loved you."

Hugh seemed almost cut to the soul by that last comment of mine. "Well I loved her very much, and I thought she did love me, too," he said after a moment's reflection, "but obviously she did not love me enough. She left me for the builder." As he said this last word, his mouth twisted, and *the builder* was like two words covered with poison that he had to spit out.

Hugh was clearly getting very emotional.

"I couldn't tell this to anybody at work, I felt such shame," he said. "It made me feel like a failure. I still don't know what made her go to another man. Was I not loving enough, was I not paying her enough attention, and were the long hours at work responsible?"

I was immediately sympathetic — and such a parallel to my own life! "Oh, I'm so sorry," I said, "such a distressing experience. No wonder you'd have difficulties trusting women after that. It's good you have no children with her. Can you imagine the heartache you would have if she left you, with two children in tow, and they would then be calling another man father? This would've been very, very difficult."

I leaned towards him and touched his hand.

He had exquisite hands with long fingers. *Well-manicured. Well, nowadays even men can have a manicure — why not if it makes them feel better? It always makes me feel better, so what's the difference?*

"Now, Hugh," I continued, starting to stroke his delicate, long-fingered hand, "all this is behind you. You are divorced, and now you can rebuild your life and find another woman to love you and have a family with you."

As I stroked his hand even more vigorously, I wanted to shout, "Forget her. Forget that you ever loved her. The proper woman is in front of you. Me, Kate. The woman you can marry and have children with. I will not leave you for a builder. Or even a plumber, for that matter."

Obviously, I couldn't be so open just half an hour into our first date. I knew I'd have to take things more slowly than that.

So I didn't say it out loud. I just thought it and looked into his eyes as I touched the little hairs on his hand, which had become erect.

"Kate," said Hugh, changing the subject, "would you like something stronger, like whisky or gin and tonic?"

"Well I like both," I said. "Do you have any preferences?"

"I prefer whisky," he said, smiling as he asked Young Pretty Waitress, who happened to be just passing our table — too frequently, I thought — for the drinks menu.

We both chose the Bruichladdich single malt. Hugh ordered doubles.

"What about your former husband?" asked Hugh, beginning his own interrogation of me. "How did your marriage finish?"

I decided that this was the time to tell him the real version of what happened, not the *He left me for his writing career in LA* version I'd developed for public consumption.

Obviously, being left for a career in Hollywood was much more romantic than being left for the barmaid with enormous tits, but this man deserved the truth.

The waitress brought our drinks, and I took a big gulp.

"Well, there is no shame in your story," I said, "cos my husband left me for a barmaid from our local," I spluttered. "I felt same way you did."

His eyes widened. He was somehow shocked with a similar story being repeated in my own marriage.

"Poor you." He held both of my hands. "I thought that such things happened only to me. And look at you — you are so attractive, like, like a princess."

I noticed that he'd already finished his whisky.

"And this scumbag husband of yours left you." He shook his head, apparently sincere in his disbelief. "Such a beautiful woman."

As he said this, he looked me in the eyes. I felt the physical attraction between us and started to wonder about what he'd be like if the two of us were somewhere private... and naked.

"Well," I sighed. "I think it happens more frequently than we imagine. Would you like more whisky?" I asked, noting his empty glass. He did and ordered two more doubles for both of us.

"Don't you need to drive?" I asked, remembering his travelling to and from work by car.

Hugh shook his head. "No," he said. "I have a flat in London and can get there by taxi. I'll call someone to bring my car to our company garage. I would never drive if I were drunk. This would invalidate my insurance, and I would need to pay for the repairs myself if I damaged my car in any way."

Well, at least he's a careful driver, not taking risks and also careful with money. So far so good.

"Hugh," I said, emptying the second double whisky, "were there any problems in your marriage in the bedroom department?"

I found myself saying these words, even though they risked upsetting him. The same question, if I'd put it to other men earlier on, would have saved a lot of trouble. I wanted to know the truth and the whole truth. I'd already had two double whiskies and felt empowered by the alcohol to find out more.

"You know," I started slurring my words, 'we might not be... err... compatible in bed." Was I going too far, talking like this on a first date? I thought of Patrick the English Language Teacher with whom I'd had a brief affair, and the heartache his *issues* had brought me. I wanted to make sure my man had nothing to hide in the bedroom department. Or that he had plenty to show off in that department. As it were...

"Oh, you mean if I'm well endowed and can perform efficiently?" He laughed, amused — and not at all embarrassed — by the question. "Yes, no problem with the size, although..."

He paused.

The last word brought me up short, just as I was about to

relax...

Ohh, so there is a problem somewhere. He cannot get it up like Patrick. Oh no, not again...

I liked this man but decided to be up front. Get any sex-related problems out on the table immediately.

"What is the problem?" I said, having gulped more whisky. It seemed that a third glass had appeared in front of me somehow, miraculously, without me noticing Hugh ordering it or the pretty waitress bringing the full glass and taking away the empty one. "Have you been to see a specialist? You know you can always take Viagra."

I was assuming much, but Hugh took it all light-heartedly.

"Oh no, no such problem," he said, laughing. "It's just that I like to fulfil some specific fantasies. Some ladies even like it. I'm into BDSM, predominantly a masochist, and I like my lady to administer punishment. Sort of sex play. Only from time to time, nothing too heavy."

Oh. Gosh. Wow. *So there is something. Life cannot be that simple.*

I gulped more of the single malt.

"Do you also do straight sex?" I enquired a moment after absorbing this news.

"Yes," said Hugh. "I do, normally after a session of being submissive, but not always. I'm very happy to have straight sex, too."

Now completely drunk on both the whisky and this information, I entered fully into the spirit of the conversation.

"Well," I said, with the serious air of someone reaching a profound conclusion on a deep philosophical question, "I think I could manage it, although I don't like to be submissive myself, and I don't like painful sex, either."

"Oh no," said Hugh, "I would never hit a woman. All the physical pain is reserved for me. You might even like it, being totally in charge." He laughed again.

I laughed with him but really wasn't sure how I felt about this. *His sexual habits seem quirky.* I'd heard that some high-powered men working in jobs where they had to make many important decisions, relaxed by pretending to be a baby. *So if he wanted me to slap his bottom, I could probably do it. Couldn't I?*

"Shall we go now?" Hugh looked at his watch.

I realised that time was marching on, and there were only a few customers still around.

"Yes, I think we should, it is quite late," I agreed swiftly.

He paid the bill and left a generous tip for the pretty waitress.

We left the café and started walking towards his car.

"It's parked nearby," explained Hugh. "I've got it in a secure underground car park. It's not exactly your run-of-the-mill charabanc, so I'm pretty careful about leaving it outside in full view of the hoi polloi."

He then took out his iPhone and pressed a speed-dial button. "Yes, Parker," he said authoritatively, "it's Mr Cartwright here. I need you to come and collect the car. You can then take it back to the company garage, as per usual. Thanks, see you shortly."

He rang off. I liked the way he'd talked to the driver. It was neither arrogant nor submissive but was clearly the confident, assertive voice of a man with money, power, and influence. A man in control of himself. A man who knew how to manage others. A man whom others would follow. A leader.

And he was handsome.

We held hands as we walked along. I felt part of a real couple. It gave me a lovely feeling of being attractive and cared for. We talked about his long hours at work and the impact that this had on his ability to find the right partner.

"You know, Kate," said Hugh, "it's not easy for me to find a good woman, who would be smart, professional, independent, who would be a person in her own right."

He suddenly stopped walking and turned to face me. I almost tripped over him, but he held me by both hands and looked deep into my eyes.

"It's really important to me," he said, "that I find the right kind of high-powered, motivated lady, who would love and accept me exactly as I am. Including my little... peccadilloes. I don't want some gold-digger, some young girl who would just feel attracted to what I can give her in a monetary sense and would only pretend to love me. I want to be loved for myself, not for my money or my lifestyle."

I was eager to give him the necessary comfort about the money. "Oh," I replied, still holding his hands and looking into his lovely eyes with matching intensity. "I know it's not easy to find the right partner. I've always been very independent financially and would never dream of relying on a man to fund my lifestyle. And I was used financially by my former husband, you know, so I'm well aware of the risk of being exploited. I totally understand your concern."

I laughed in a tone that I hoped was empathetic, supportive. "I wouldn't date a man who doesn't have a good job," I continued, "who isn't independent and high-powered himself. I want to learn from my mistake in my first marriage. I don't want to repeat it."

As I said this, I recalled my brief affair with Patrick, the definitely not high-powered lowly English teacher at the college. And my not-so-brief affair with Paul the Spy, which ended so badly. Both were clear examples of my not learning from my mistakes. I hastily pushed the memories aside and concentrated on Hugh.

He seemed pleased with my response. He didn't move and continued to hold my hands tightly.

"That's good, that's good," he said. "We have the same values. And I'm not really into trying to find a partner by going to clubs and picking up girls. The sex might be okay, but it never leads anywhere. They just want me to buy them drinks and jewellery."

The mention of other girls, and even the idea of him having sex with them, caused me to feel a frisson of jealousy and excitement at the same time.

He let go of one of my hands, turned to one side, and we then started walking forward again.

"So I'm really not into clubbing," continued Hugh. "As a matter of fact, I can get very sleepy quite early in the evening. Staying up late into the night drinking ain't my cup of tea. My mind has to be very fresh and alert in the morning when the markets open. The bank and my clients make investments based on my decisions. There's a lot of money at stake, and I'm under a lot of pressure from early morning to late."

We reached his car. It was an expensive Bugatti Chiron.

This guy makes some serious cash. I admired its sleek outline and the sense of power and energy it projected, even while silent and still. *Nought to sixty in seven seconds. No wonder he doesn't want to drive it while drunk. And no wonder he's worried about being taken for a ride by some girl wanting him for his cash. There are probably women out there who'd shag him in a heartbeat just for the chance to be seen in the Bugatti.*

Hugh opened the passenger door and motioned for me to get inside.

"Kate," he said, "please get in, you're shivering in the cold. I'll put the heating on, and we can get you warm."

So I slid in and settled my bottom into the most glorious leather car seat I'd ever experienced. My nose twitched. The scent and sensation of the leather almost had me coming by itself.

And I've a lovely, sexy, handsome, successful male as my companion in this car. What's making me more excited, the car or the man?

Both equally, I decided.

Hugh closed the passenger door and walked round to the other side. He opened that door, too, and got into the driver's seat. He turned on the engine, which roared, as only a small sports car with an eight-litre engine can roar. The powerful engine made the car vibrate, and some of the vibrations found their way into my body.

It felt good. *More than good...*

Hugh turned on the heating, and warm air emerged from the vents. He turned and smiled at me.

"That'll warm the cockles," he said.

I put my left hand towards the source of the heat to warm it up. Hugh took my right hand and started blowing on my fingers.

"Just to help warm it up," he commented. "We can't have one hand feeling better than the other."

The tiny puffs of air from his mouth turned into small kisses on my fingers and later on the top of my hand.

So there I was, dressed in silk and cashmere, sitting in the ultra-high quality leather seat of a car that retailed for — well, I wasn't sure how much the car cost, but it was obviously a lot more than some beaten-up old Ford — with this gorgeous man... and the electrical current of sexual attraction between us was palpable.

I looked at him as he kissed my hand. I wanted to thank him for the good job he was doing warming my hand up. However, my attention was taken by the way he'd changed from kissing the fingers to licking the space between them. He did it very delicately, and I became transfixed by the process and by the feeling.

I was a bit drunk, that was undoubtedly the case, but that was not the reason why my heart was beating more loudly and quickly than usual, nor could it explain why my silk knickers were a little on the damp side.

Has he noticed the effect his presence is having on my body?

Has he realised that I'm intensely attracted to him?

Then I suddenly remembered Hugh's comments about women who were after him for his money. I felt embarrassed...

So I withdrew my hand. I didn't want Hugh to think that I was after his money or his car. I felt that I couldn't really show him how attracted I was to him. He might interpret it the wrong way.

Pity, he is gorgeous.

"Hugh," I said, almost primly. "I need to go. I'm very warm now, thank you. And thank you for the lovely date, I really enjoyed meeting you."

Shall I ask him for another date? No, this would be much too forward. I need to behave like a lady, be sweet and be appreciative but allow him to take the initiative regarding future dates.

But Hugh didn't seem to want to let it go.

"Oh no, don't go yet, Kate," he protested.

I looked at him and saw his eyes pleading with me.

Was he as attracted to me as much as I was attracted to him?

Now he got hold of both my hands and pulled me towards him while leaning forward at the same time.

Maybe I don't need to worry about being regarded as a gold-digger after all. His mouth got close to mine. *I think I'll just go with the flow.*

So I didn't protest, and soon his lips were on mine. We kissed, gently to begin with and then more intensely. I gave as good as I got. Hugh obviously noticed I was up for it and started exploring my mouth, pushing his tongue in deeply. I had to admit, he was a good kisser, and I could feel my body reacting to his kisses and his touch. I was getting very aroused. I started to moan as the excitement built. The idea of being taken in one of the world's most luxurious cars was so thrilling. I wanted to be naked as quickly as possible and lifted my legs up in preparation for removing my tiny silky panties.

Suddenly, there was a loud knock on the door. Our lips parted at the sound, and I abandoned my task of panty removal.

Hugh coughed and said, "Who's there?"

"Parker, Mr Cartwright, sir," said the voice of a young man.

The driver had arrived.

Hugh replied, "Ah, yes, Parker, that's good, you're here."

Hugh opened his door, and I saw a young man standing next to the car, wearing a chauffeur's uniform.

Shit, had he seen us kissing?

We'd gone a touch beyond kissing...

I noticed that the windows were blacked out, so he probably hadn't seen us.

Well, Parker had come a bit too soon, which means that neither Hugh nor I had come at all...

I really wouldn't have minded sampling Hugh's kisses for a bit longer.

Hugh got out of the car, smoothing down his slightly dishevelled hair as he did so. Nodding to Parker, Hugh rushed round to my side and opened the door for me. I got out and glanced at Parker.

I really tried to avoid appearing sheepish when I caught Parker's eye. He was quite handsome himself and was evidently trying to make his grin less obvious, in an attempt to persuade his boss and the boss's lady companion that he had no idea what we'd been doing.

I was pleased to note that Parker gave me a brief look of appreciation. I was perhaps to be regarded as a fit companion for the boss.

Well, that's a redeeming feature of interrupting our in-car coitus-to-come. Albeit the only one.

Hugh handed over his car keys to the grinning driver and soon the Bugatti disappeared out of sight.

"Well," said Hugh, "I'll have to go to work tomorrow by taxi but I didn't want to take any risks, really." Hugh was a bit grumpy and not at all happy at parting with his car.

He turned towards me, and his mood changed.

"Now," he said, holding me tightly to him, so I could feel you-know-what hard against my midriff. "I need to get a taxi to my place. I live in Point West on Gloucester Road, would you like to come? And perhaps pick up where we left off?"

What? He wants me to go to his place now? Is he looking for a girlfriend and a future wife or just a one-night stand, like with those girls from the clubs? Would sex on the first date prejudice any sort of future relationship development? Should I risk it?

I was well aroused myself and a bit of relief would be good, but I didn't want to jeopardise the relationship, which had started to develop quite nicely. Even our brief commencement in the car had made me think he was sexually adept.

It would be good to continue at his place...

Suddenly I remembered what he'd told me in the café about being a submissive. What if, once we were at his flat, he wanted me to do some strange things to him and I failed miserably? The possibility of a relationship with him would be rendered null and void. I couldn't risk it for the sake of a quick orgasm. *My vibrator will deal with that, thank you.* I needed to learn a bit more about this lovely man in front of me and about his unusual, and very specific, needs and desires, before being alone with him for sex.

"Well," I said, "better not this time, Hugh, I've an early start tomorrow. I'll take the Tube to my house. Thank you for the invitation anyway." I kissed him lightly on the cheek and thanked him again for this evening.

He had a quick look at his watch, presumably taking note of the time.

"All right, Kate," he said. "I suppose it's a bit late, and I do have an early start tomorrow as well."

He smiled and took me in his arms and kissed me.

"We're definitely meeting again," he said. "I'm not about to let someone as lovely as you slip away. I'll be in touch."

He walked me to the Tube station, kissed me on the cheek, and promised to call me. The train arrived quickly. I sat down and thought about the events of the evening.

I decided that it had been a wise decision not to go to his place. I hadn't wanted to seem too keen, and this whole submissive thing was a worry. We would end up in bed, maybe he'd ask me to spank him, and I really felt that there was a risk of me simply being unable to do it properly. Then if I stayed there overnight he would be getting up very early in the morning and preparing for work. There wouldn't be time to discuss the submissive thing, and there'd be a pall over the whole night.

So on the whole, a wise decision not to go with him.

Then I suddenly realised that tomorrow was Saturday, so perhaps we could have had a night of lovemaking and stayed in bed in the morning. We could have resolved any issues arising out of the submissive thing then and there. *Maybe he'd even serve me breakfast. If that were all that was involved in being submissive, I'd be happy with that.*

So perhaps it was not so wise a decision and I should have accepted his offer. Well, too late now.

No, silly me, it was the right decision.

He could have thought that I was either too easy or too much attracted to his money, even if the submissive thing turned out not to be an issue.

Remember, Kate, he is looking for a life partner, like you are, and you should not end up in the category of a one-night stand only.

I needed to respect myself and make him do the running. Our relationship needed to develop further before we went to bed and made love.

But I went to bed on the first night with Luciano, and that is still going on. He didn't dump me after the sex on our first date, did he?

Well, Luciano was off limits and not suitable as a life partner. The sexual relationship—now a little less frequent than previously—was benefiting both of us. I hadn't fallen in love with him knowing that he couldn't be placed in the *possible husband* category.

Yes, Hugh definitely was possible husband material, but I had to tread carefully. I would also need a bit more research on the *submissive* aspect. This was a new one on me, and I needed to ensure that I could deal with it before engaging in sex with him, and certainly before becoming too emotionally involved.

Would he want some sort of role play in the bedroom? I would be the mum or the teacher punishing a naughty boy by slapping his buttocks. Would this satisfy him? Could I even manage that? What if he wanted something more... difficult?

What a lovely man he is anyway.

I got off the train holding the bunch of red roses he'd given me. We had a similar divorce background—we both were treated badly by our former spouses. He was obviously a high flyer, and I could see why women would be attracted to his lifestyle. Yet he was aware of it and was looking for a partner who would value him as a human being. He seemed very genuine while telling me all of this on our first date.

But this thing about being a submissive, what does he really need from me?

It suddenly dawned on me that if he was a submissive, I'd have to be a Dominatrix. How? What would he want me to do to him? Would I know how to do it?

Well, this'll be something new to learn.

I liked being in control of my life—being in control of the

sex session could be fun. Couldn't it?

Anyway, he does straight sex, too—he told me that, so it might be easier than I think. I was a sex goddess now, after all, and quite well-educated in such matters thanks to Luciano's efforts. I reached my front door and after a short visit to the loo took my vibrator out of the cupboard where it had been quietly and patiently waiting for me.

Well, straight sex with a vibrator, what a pleasure!

I thought of Hugh kissing my lips and going down on my body, cupping my breasts with his lovely hands and kissing the rosebuds on the top of my bare breasts. I felt my nipples getting erect just at the thought of it. Then, in my imagination, Hugh kissed my belly, moving on to my inner thighs, and coming soon to kissing my nether lips and progressing to little kisses on my clitoris.

"Oh, Hugh, you are fantastic," I screamed, the vision of him clear in my head. The vision was nearly as good as the reality could be, and the orgasm had come immediately.

Relaxed and happy, I went to bed thinking about my new man and all the possibilities this could bring into my life. I had no dreams that night and woke up refreshed and in a great mood.

* * * *

I spent the weekend with my sister's family playing with my little niece, Olivia, and daydreaming of a man like John, my brother-in-law. He was attentive and loving towards Ann, and I imagined Hugh standing next to me and behaving in the same loving way towards me. I saw myself feeling happy and holding a small baby girl in my arms.

Hugh called me on Sunday afternoon, just after lunch. I told him I was at my sister's place and there wasn't much opportunity for a long conversation. He was keen to arrange another date, and I welcomed this, although I still wanted to appear a little aloof. Just a touch—it wasn't easy sticking to that narrow path that lies between the lands of So Hard to Get That He Gives Up and Take Me Now I'm Yours.

I told him that I'd call him back tomorrow, Monday, once I knew my schedule for the coming week, and we would arrange a date.

He happily agreed to this, so my approach must have worked. In fact, *all* my evenings the next week were free, as the only person who kept me busy in the evening was Luciano, and he was away on a business trip. Or else busy servicing other female members of the Luciano Stable of Lucky Fillies.

But that didn't bother me, Luciano was a free agent, and so was I. And Hugh's call had proved that he was interested in continuing our relationship despite my refusal to go to his place, and notwithstanding the fact that our attempt at Sex in a Bugatti had been interrupted by the chauffeur.

My sister noticed the telephone call. She looked at me quizzically, smiled enigmatically, and said, with an excessively casual air, "New boyfriend, Kate?"

I tried to match her casual, relaxed manner by replying with, "Oh", tossing the mobile phone in the air and then dropping it. "I just started dating this guy. He seems terribly nice, very rich and successful, and drives a very nice expensive car."

"What car does he drive?" John chipped in, looking up with considerable interest in his eyes.

"Oh really, John," said Ann primly, "what matters is Kate's happiness. You should be asking about his character, not about the damn automobile."

John laughed and continued. "But, Ann, Kate's already said that he's nice, so that's enough on his character for my purposes. Any more would be intrusive."

That last comment was a mild rebuke to Ann. John felt

that Ann's sisterly questions about my sex and love life strayed into Spanish Inquisition territory sometimes. Once when I was answering detailed questions about Patrick — the English teacher with a masturbation problem I'd dated briefly — John had accused Ann of being *little more than a modern-day Torquemada.*

Ann bristled at the term *intrusive* but didn't reply. So it seemed that the car issue had to be addressed.

"Oh," I said, trying to sound casual, "some sort of Italian sports car, leather interior, very loud engine. Hugh seemed very attached to it. A Bugatti Chiron, I think."

John leapt up as if someone had inserted an electric cattle prod into his bottom. His glass of wine was waved wildly in the air, and some of its contents spilt onto the Persian rug on which he'd been sitting, playing peek-a-boo with Olivia.

"Bugatti!" he spluttered. "Bugatti? Are you sure?"

His face had turned puce. The expression on his face was a strange blend of emotions — joy at the idea of a Bugatti, and jealousy at the idea of a Bugatti being owned by someone other than him.

John did love his cars.

"Of course I'm sure," I said. "You've taught me enough about cars, John, for me to know a Bugatti Chiron from a Ford Fiesta."

John seemed to calm slightly at the implication that my knowledge on this specialist subject was all down to his tutelage.

"Three million quid! That's how much a car like that costs! Three million smackers! More than the cost of the whole street we're in," he said. "Cripes, Kate, who are you shagging? The CEO of Google? Some duke who owns half of Scotland? A Colombian drug baron?"

Then for a moment he looked intrigued. "You didn't have sex actually inside the Bugatti, did you?" he said, eyes bulging.

I chose not to address the bit about shagging in the car but instead focussed on dispelling myths about my prospective beau.

"Hugh is none of those," I said. "He's an English commodities trader. I suppose he's a big cheese at some bank or brokerage or whatever. He works very hard, long hours."

I didn't mention the bit about being a submissive. Something told me that this aspect of Hugh would worry Ann and lead to unhelpful ribaldry from John. And there was no chance, I felt, that either of them would actually know enough about sadomasochism to help me understand what it was all about.

"Look," I said. "Hugh and I have only been on one date so far. Another's been arranged. There's not much to discuss yet. I'll keep you posted." I looked at John. "Especially regarding the car."

* * * *

I got back from my sister's house late in the evening on Sunday and decided to go straight to bed. As I lay there, I realised that I needed to do a bit of internet research on the subject of sadomasochism, being a submissive, etcetera. I knew that I needed to learn more from others.

And I needed to ask Hugh what he really expected me to do. If anything. Maybe I was exaggerating the whole thing, *over-thinking* this submissive stuff. He was evidently a good kisser and got aroused easily without any need for slapping him, so hopefully it could boil down to me lightly smacking his bare bum while he pounded away inside me.

This last thought contented me but also brought forth some tension down below. I reached across to the bedside drawer and brought out my most faithful friend, the Rampant Rabbit vibrator. A few minutes later, some pennies-worth of battery power consumed, and I was satisfied. As, in my imagination, was Hugh.

* * * *

Next day at the office, I busied myself with all the urgent work on my desk. Things were going well with the Marketing Department, and there was no doubt that the young Chinese girl recently transferred to my team was starting to produce the goods. Several hundred emails had been sent out in Mandarin characters to college addresses in huge Chinese cities I'd never heard of, and we'd already had expressions of interest from several about sending students over for English language teaching.

Andy had taken the Chinese girl under his wing, and she was clearly too busy to spend lots of time in the boss's office, mini-skirted and giggling orientally.

So it was only at lunch time that I realised that I still had to do my research on submissive men.

Should I Google it? On the work computer or on my phone?

I started looking for my mobile and panicked when I couldn't find it, neither in my handbag nor anywhere in the office.

Then I realised that I'd left it at my sister's house. *Crap.* I'd been too preoccupied thinking about Hugh.

I cursed my own lack of attention to details like keeping my mobile phone in my handbag. I became distracted and couldn't concentrate on work at all.

Double crap.

How am I going to call Hugh if his number is only stored on my mobile? What would happen if I lost my mobile completely and he kept calling me and getting no reply? He might think that I didn't want anything to do with him. I can't risk losing this lovely man.

The prospect was so awful that I resolved immediately that there would be full-blown explosive sex at our next meeting, lots of it. No more aloofness.

I called my sister, and she found my mobile in the sitting room where I'd left it.

Relief.

"Ann," I said, "that's great, I was worried. I need my mobile for work. I'll come straight from the office to collect it. Is that all right?"

"Oh, Kate, don't worry. I'm going to collect Olivia from her pre-school. I've got your spare house key, don't forget. I'll drop your mobile off at your place. I'll put it on the kitchen table, so you can go straight home. You must be tired after the whole day at work, no need to come to our place first."

What a treasure my sister can be. And I told her so.

So the case of the missing phone was solved. I would be able to call Hugh as soon as I got home.

My thoughts reverted to researching sadomasochism. I needed to find out more about all this. However, doing the required searches on my work computer was totally out of the question. The guy from the IT department, who, I suspected, was already monitoring all my emails, would have a field day should he check the searches.

The consequential inquisition I'd face from the boss would be uncomfortable, to say the least.

I'd read somewhere that even after deleting your search history the IT specialist can still see what you were watching. He was a very sleazy customer, and I didn't want any gossip about my sexual habits.

Fine, I could wait until I got home, but I decided to have a chat with the only confidant I had in the office, my lovely gay assistant, Andy.

I knew he would never divulge any of my secrets.

* * * *

I signalled to Andy to close the door, indicating that we were about to have one of our *confidential chats*. He grinned excitedly and strode over to the door, closing it theatrically, as if he were a secret agent on a mission.

"Andy, listen," I said when he was back in his seat, with his *I'm all ears* look on his face. "I met a guy who says that he is a submissive and I have no idea what he would want me to do. I don't feel comfortable hitting him," I continued, "but I don't want to be considered" — I struggled for the right word — "backwards in the sexual area. It seems to be nowadays accepted as normal behaviour. What do you think?"

"Oh, well..." Andy started laughing. "Have you read any of the Marquis de Sade books?"

"No, I haven't," I said, irritated but intrigued by Andy's immediate recourse to classical French literature as the best place to begin our discussion. "Can I learn anything practical from them?"

"Practical?" said Andy. "No, not so much the practical aspects of sadomasochism, more of the philosophy behind it."

Philosophy? How come there's a philosophy behind hitting someone for sexual kicks?

"You see," he said, as if he were the Professor of Sado-masochism at the University of Fucking, "some people want to be in control, and some want to be controlled. This applies to sexual situations as much as in real life. And there are guys who spend hours being in control in business who need the release of being a submissive."

He leaned back in his chair with the air of a top academic who had just delivered himself of an intellectual bon mot.

I thought about this for a moment.

"Oh," I said. "I'm okay being in control of a man, no problem. My whole life seems out of control sometimes, so a bit of being in charge wouldn't do me any harm at all. No,

Andy, that's not the issue. What I'm afraid of is that I'll be useless, not knowing what to say or what to do. Practically. I might just start laughing and not take the whole thing seriously."

"Well, that wouldn't do at all," said Prof Andy sternly. "This is like an acting performance. You can't play Desdemona and then start laughing at Iago. You need to be self-disciplined enough to take it seriously, or your partner will feel humiliated." He paused. "Let me think about it. I might be able to help."

He left the room. He came back about forty minutes later.

"Kate," he said. "I've got you a contact number to someone who can teach you about all this." He handed me a business card with a telephone number on it and a silhouette of a buxom lady holding a whip in the air. "This lady works as a Dominatrix."

No shit, Sherlock. I looked at the card.

"What, a prostitute?" I said, startled. "You want me to have lessons from a prostitute?"

"Depends what you call prostitution," said Andy, back in his professorial mode. "Yes, the client does pay her, but she doesn't sleep with them, she dominates them, and they get sort of sexual pleasure out of this."

I was confused. "This is weird, Andy. My guy said he wants to be dominated as he is a submissive, but he also does straight sex."

"Well, Kate," said Andy. "I really think that if you want to pursue a relationship with this guy, you're gonna have to find out if you're comfortable with his... peccadilloes... and this is a very good way of discovering if you have an... Inner Mistress within yourself. As it were. Anyway, nothing ventured, nothing gained. Think about it. You've got the number."

He went back to his desk and returned to the more prosaic task of checking whether all our Kazakh students had paid their fees.

* * * *

Now after this conversation with Andy, I was in two minds. Should I get a lesson as a Dominatrix from a lady of the night or should I go further into the relationship, fall in love and then be left by my man if I turn out to be useless in being his... Mistress and slapping him the wrong way?

What's the right way to hit someone, anyway? Should I really be getting into a relationship with someone who enjoys being slapped?

I thought of Hugh and his hazel eyes, his beautiful hands, his exciting kisses, and decided that I needed to try. If I didn't, I would regret it later. What if I just gave up at the first hurdle and missed my chance with him? I could meet him a few years later with a lovely wife on his arm and two lovely children while having none of my own. He wanted a wife and children, I remembered. And as for his... peccadillo, as Andy — and Hugh himself — called it, well, it might not be so bad.

"You might even like it." I remembered Hugh's statement and heard him laughing.

Coming home, I found my mobile on my kitchen table and a lovely note from Ann.

Kate,
Thank you for being lovely company for the weekend.

She was right about that. I'd been very well-behaved. I'd never mentioned the Scumbag, my former husband, even once, and I'd not cried about my failed relationship with Paul the Customs Spy, who'd dumped me for his ex-wife.

This is a good change.

Ann's note continued.

We both wish you all the best with the new man.
And, Kate, remember I am always here for you if you need to talk.
Ann xx

I was touched. *My dear sister, being such a rock when my marriage failed.* I was grateful to have her in my life. *And my mum, too.* My lovely mum, hardly ever at home, always a workaholic, even now when she didn't need to work so hard.
Should I discuss my hunt for a husband with Mum?
Hmmm. *No, matters of the heart are better discussed with Ann. I can't ever involve Mum in any of this.*
I switched the television on while reheating the pre-prepared dinner I'd taken out of the freezer in the morning. I needed to call Hugh later. My mind went again to my date. And I needed to do my critically important research on the internet.
Anything was possible, I supposed, as I sat in front of the TV eating my dinner and watching an episode of *Sexcetera* in which women stripped naked and pretended to be ponies in harnesses while being led around the street—in summer, I should add—by their *owners*.
I finished my dinner and decided to call Hugh—after all, this was what I'd promised to him yesterday. At that very moment my phone rang, and I saw Hugh's name.
I pressed the Accept button and said, "Wow, Hugh, I was about to call you, what a coincidence."
"Hi, Kate, are you free to talk?" Hugh asked politely. "I wasn't sure if it was you to call me or vice versa, so I decided to take the initiative and call you. How are you? How was your day at work? Busy?"
"Yes, quite busy," I replied brightly. "Thank you for ask-

ing. We're preparing a big advertising campaign for China. It's a great market for British education, and we hope to enrol a good number of students from there."

True, but dull. So I changed the subject.

"Anyway, that's enough about me. How was your day? Good?"

"Good," he said, "but very busy and very tiring. I just got home. I started at six am, so it's been a long day."

I looked at the clock.

Blimey, it's half past eight, so he spent fourteen hours at work? Much too long.

"You are working too hard, Hugh," I said sympathetically. "Have you ever thought of changing jobs?"

He laughed. "Yes, I have. The next job will be Being a Beach Bum. I'm planning to retire at forty and enjoy life. Just a few more years to go, though."

He coughed, with a touch of nervousness. "Well, Kate," he said, "I really enjoyed our date last week, and I was wondering if I could invite you for dinner to the Ritz this Saturday. I'll be a bit busy during the week, but the weekend is free, and I would love to see you again."

Oh goody.

"Yes, of course, Hugh," I replied eagerly. "I would be happy to go to dinner with you, and I love the Ritz. Not that I've been there much."

"Great," said Hugh, "all sorted, then. I'll see you on Saturday. Must rush now, I've a client dinner at the Savoy. Looking forward to seeing you on Saturday at the Ritz."

He hung up.

Well, he's invited me to the Ritz. This is very posh, isn't it? I'd been there only once for a drink with a friend, never for dinner.

Ritz, that's very upper crust, very conservative, maybe I'll see Prince Charles there, together with Camilla.

Suddenly, I remembered Prince Charles's great-uncle,

King Edward VIII, and the affair with Wallis Simpson. I'd heard that she was a Dominatrix and that was why he was so much in love with her.

I wanted my new man to love me and be totally devoted to me. *Can I be as skilful as Mrs Simpson was?* He resigned from being the king for her. What a sacrifice to make for love.

I made my mind up. Well, the things you do for love, true love. I called the number on the card Andy had given me. It went straight into answer phone. I left my number and asked for a call back.

She rang ten minutes later.

"Oh hi, I'm Mistress Ulrika. You left a message to call you. Are you interested in buying a session for your partner or a lesson for yourself? I only specialise in dominating men. Should you require a session for yourself, I can refer you to a friend of mine." She had a deep voice with a slight foreign accent, German perhaps.

"I-I want to learn from you, you know... My new partner admitted that he likes to be submissive, and I have no idea what to do." I was stuttering, feeling somehow embarrassed telling her this quite intimate story.

"That's fine. Lessons are cheaper." Her tone was crisp and business-like, a real professional.

She went through a few practical things, named the price for the lesson, gave me her address, and laid down some basic rules.

"Obviously no recordings, no hidden cameras on your body, and you would need to sign a non-disclosure agreement as you would be taking part in a real-life session and my client's identity must be protected. You will be protected yourself by wearing a mask, so my client will not recognise you. And, please, no introductions with your real name."

Blimey, is she a lawyer in her spare time?

"Oh, I would never say anything to anybody," I began to

reply.

She cut me off curtly. "We have our reputation to think of, and we need to protect our clients. Your identity has to be protected, too. You need to sign the non-disclosure before we can proceed," she insisted.

I started to understand why she was a Dominatrix—she was authoritative, and the tonality of her voice was such that you felt compelled to obey. I felt quite dominated by her already. I relented and agreed to her demands.

"Okay," I said, "if it is necessary, I will sign it."

She seemed to relax, and the tone of her voice became much softer.

"Do you have your Dominatrix outfit?" was her next question to me.

I was flummoxed by this. "What is it?" I asked, confused. "Do I need it for the lesson?"

"Well, obviously you don't have one, then," she said. "We will lend you one of ours, including the mask to hide your face, and tell you where you can buy them. This will be real on-the-job training."

Sounds good. I guess...

"When do you want to come for the lesson?" Ulrika continued.

"Any evening after six this week if possible?" I decided to get the training ASAP, before Saturday, anyway.

"Well, we are pretty booked in the evenings. The nearest date for an evening training session is available in three weeks. If you want anything earlier I have an opening this Friday, lunch time."

Yes, ma'am!

"Oh, that's fine, I'll be there."

"Yes, but before we can book you in we would require payment in advance. You can pay by bank transfer or credit or debit card. On the statement it will appear as *Dominos Ltd*. Please come on time as I need to go through some points with you before the client comes, so you will know how to use the equipment in the dungeon and will not damage your man while trying anything on your own."

Bloody hell. So there is equipment required. What sort of equipment?

I suddenly remembered my dream about the Regency lord and the book which inspired it. I'd nearly forgotten about all that, but now I remembered the ropes and the whips. I shuddered.

"How do you want to pay?" Ulrika's voice brought me back to reality.

I paid by credit card to *Dominos Ltd*, and the conversation ended.

I forgot to ask Ulrika if I'd be offered a real fuck from the client as a bonus. Could I refuse if I didn't fancy him? This would obviously have been a joke, but the stern demeanour adopted by Ulrika implied that this joke question would offend her professional sensibilities. Perhaps it was for the best that I hadn't asked.

I was going to get some education about the world of BDSM. I was going to be in training, an intern in the world of Dominatrices and their clients. This was scary yet exciting. Would I be aghast or excited? I remembered my dream and remembered how appalled I was when the Regency lord hit the poor doppelganger of mine on her breasts. Well, here it was going to be the opposite—a man being hit by a woman.

A man being hit by me. Golly gosh.

The words—dungeon, Dominatrix, pain, sadomasochism—were rattling around in my head. I went to bed and tried to read a new novel I'd bought recently— rather boring, it was. It was just a straightforward love story, nothing special. The difficulties in the relationship were all around his family, mother, and grandmother not accepting the young woman in his life and her trying to overcome their prejudices.

Typical, same as many books on the subject. Nothing like the real-life love story I was embarking on—an exciting new world of fetishes, domination, and sexual gratification in an unusual way.

Maybe I should write my own book about my journey.

I put the book away and fell asleep.

* * * *

The dream came to me in the early hours of the morning. My last recollection before dozing off was of the rain striking hard on the windowpane, making me move farther down the bed, well underneath my warm duvet. And then...

I was in a dungeon, a poky dark underground room with all sorts of strange equipment lurking in its corners. I felt quite at home there, and my dream-self felt very much in control of the situation. I stared down at myself and noticed that I was dressed head to toe in a tight black shiny leather costume. My lower legs were encased in black thigh-high boots with very high stiletto heels. I was wearing a black leather glove on my right hand. The back of the glove seemed to be encrusted with tiny crystals, which flashed in the candlelight.

I was breathing hard, as if I had started the dream in the midst of an enormous physical effort, like I'd been running a marathon. I glanced again at my gloved right hand. The fingers enclosed a black whip which was smeared with some viscous substance. Its colour was indistinguishable against the whip's darkness. But my dream-self knew what it was. It was blood. Human blood. The blood of my victim.

I raised the whip and brought it down with a loud shout on the bare, bloodied back of a masked, but otherwise naked, man, who was tied up to something which looked like a cross. The sound I made as I brought the whip down with all my strength was half born of effort, half of fury, as if my dream-self felt keenly the justice of the severe punishment I was inflicting.

The man being whipped was apparently not having fun. Whether he, too, shared my sense of his punishment being well-deserved was unclear, because he was fully engaged in crying out from the pain and begging me, quite unsuccessfully, for mercy.

I raised the whip again, and it struck him across the buttocks with a satisfying thwack. *It appeared that my dream-self was quite adept at this activity. I was obviously fully wound up into the physical rhythm of the whipping. I whipped him hard, three times in succession, before having to stop to draw breath.*

I felt disgusted with my dream-self, who was obviously not at all ashamed or embarrassed by what was being done in this dark cell.

Actually, my dream-self felt good about this. I did not know that I had in me such capacity for cruelty to another human being, but whipping him with such severity made me feel empowered and in control.

I realised that I actually enjoyed being in charge of the situation. I felt fabulous. Although I had no knowledge of the specifics of the crime committed by this man, my dream-self knew that his crimes were many and dreadful, and fully deserving of the sentence he had doubtless received before being handed to me, to be stripped naked, masked, and whipped until the blood ran and then whipped some more.

Suddenly the masked man spoke. It was not, of course, the calm discourse of a man sitting in an armchair, waiting for his woman to get dressed. He was screaming and crying.

"Please, please, Mistress Kate," this pathetic criminal shouted out. "Please stop, I am sorry, I am so sorry. Please stop, I beg you!"

But my dream-self was immune to his begging. In fact, it seemed to infuriate me. "Beg me more!" I yelled, hitting him harder, and he did.

"I am so sorry, Mistress Kate. I am sorry I betrayed you, I am sorry I caused you so much pain. Please forgive me, I am sorry... I regret what I did to you."

He was crying and begging for my *forgiveness. What was it* that I was personally to forgive him for, what betrayal to me specifically? Surely this man, this evil-doer, had been sentenced to a whipping at my House of Pain for crimes against humanity generally, not just against me personally?

I was confused but didn't want to stop hitting him. My dream-self knew that the sentence needed to be implemented, and in full. There was no room for mercy, that would be to transfer the punishment from this degenerate to his victim or victims, and that would simply compound the injustice, rather than remove it.

My dream-self remembered the specifics of the judgment which brought this villain to my dungeon. I was determined, almost delighted, to obey the injunction in detail. So I walked over to him, letting the whip hang loosely in my gloved hand. I seized his chin with my left hand and squeezed.

"You remember the judge's words, don't you, pond life?" my dream-self snarled, his jawbone almost cracking in my unyielding grip. "You recall what comes next? To ensure you never treat another woman the way you treated your victim."

The man seemed to nod, although his head's movement was constrained by what I was doing to his mouth. I let go of his chin to let him speak.

He squealed in a thin voice. "I know I deserve it, Mistress Kate. Thank you, Mistress Kate."

"Now then, dirtbag," I said. "I will untie you. You will then turn round and allow yourself to be retied to this most excellent post for the final stage of your punishment."

I untied his hands and feet from the cross, as the blood on his back still ran down from the blows I'd inflicted. His head was bowed. He made no attempt to resist me as I tied him back again, wrists and ankles, but this time facing me.

I stood back briefly to admire my work. There was, as yet, no blood on his front. I stared, transfixed momentarily by the state of his manhood. I noted, with pleasure, its shrunken pathetic state and the way the balls hung below. I knew that, in the course of committing his crimes, he'd been naked under different circumstances, his manhood engorged, his orgasm imminent.

So what is to follow is not merely just, it is a punishment that fits the crime.

But first a little more whipping on his bum, so I can extend his pain for a little longer.

So cracking the whip rhythmically on the floor, I marched around the whipping post to his back. Then, I delivered three more smart whacks to his bottom. He convulsed but did not speak.

I marched back to his front.

The moment of total justice has come, the moment of catharsis and release for me.

I held the whip high above my head, and with all the strength I could muster, I hit him on his genitals.

He yelled, and his body convulsed. I gave it ten seconds before hitting him there again, right in the balls. And then I gave it ten more seconds before giving him what he so richly deserved for the third, and final, time.

Exactly as the lady judge ordained at the trial. *My dream-self recalled that with satisfaction. I remembered her words, spoken with such relish, "The three whips on your cock and balls shall be subject to ten-second intervals, so that any numbing can subside, with the intention that each strike shall inflict new pain, to be experienced anew, so that you shall remember to the end of your disgusting days the pain you inflicted on an innocent woman."*

As she completed this stern pronouncement, I heard cheers from what was apparently the jury. Twelve women, of full age, good and true citizens of our land. All of whom had shouted, with one voice, the single word guilty *when the judge had sonorously asked them for their verdict against this vile criminal.*

I felt empowered. I felt good. I could have hit him more, the judgement allowed me, as executioner, that latitude, but I was satiated. I had no need to hit him anymore.

The crime was punishment enough.

So I stopped, came towards the whimpering man, and ripped his mask off.

Underneath was the face of my Scumbag ex-husband, crying

and still begging my forgiveness.

Good grief. I woke up with a jerk, sweating, the sheet and duvet soaked with my perspiration.

It was early morning, and I was in my bed and not in the dungeon. Going back to sleep was no longer possible. I was thinking about the dream and the Scumbag's face full of pain.

Well, this is what I should've done when I saw the two of them together. Whip him — and her — until they started bleeding. That would have taught him a damn good lesson. He left me with a bleeding heart. He deserved a real beating for what he'd done to me.

Harsh, but fair. I didn't feel sorry for the Scumbag. He deserved a good beating. Anyway, it was just a dream. *What a pity!*

Despite how I'd felt during the dream's final second, the dream had actually made me feel good. It made me feel empowered. It made me feel that I could get justice in the real world for how I'd been treated by the Scumbag, albeit that revenge would take the form of a loving, devoted husband and family, rather than whipping the Scumbag into oblivion.

Maybe Hugh could be The One. *We shall see.* I started looking forward to the lesson with Mistress Ulrika.

* * * *

I needed to find out more about Hugh's peccadilloes. So I settled down at my home computer and typed the BDSM abbreviation into ever-reliable Google.

At this point, I really had only the vaguest notion of what those four letters stood for. I needed to understand better. I could have asked Andy, but he was an unforgiving teacher when dealing with an honest, but ignorant, seeker after knowledge like myself. My not having read any Marquis De

Sade stories seemed to result in him addressing me as if I were not his boss, but rather a naughty schoolboy in the *Remove at Eton* who needed to be humiliated for his ignorance of Horace's iambic poems in front of the whole class. There was only so much of the Billy Bunter treatment that I could take from Andy.

There were numerous pages listed on the search result. I opened the first link and read the BDSM definition.

BDSM is a continuum of erotic practice and expression involving the consensual use of restraint, intense sensory stimulation, and fantasy power role-play. The compound acronym, BDSM, is derived from the terms bondage and discipline (B&D or B/D), Dominance and submission (D&S or D/s), and sadism and masochism (S&M or S/M).
B – Bondage
D – Dominance
S – Sadism
M – Masochism

Crikey, sexuality reduced to a chemical formula. Well, that's Wikipedia for you, thorough but shorn of emotion.
At least I had a definition I could understand, and I could now use that term without worrying about being caught ignorant of what it meant.

Now I started Googling *submissive man in BDSM practice.*

Again Wikipedia had the answer.

Male submission describes BDSM *and other* sexual activities *in which the* submissive *partner is male, and may be referred to as* servant. *It generally refers to sexual activities and desires in which a male-identified person, such as a man, plays a subservient role to a Dominant partner. The term* male submissive *and its abbreviation malesub are widely used in* BDSM *subcultures to refer to such a person. The female Dominant counterpart is abbrevi-*

ated femdom, while the male Dominant counterpart is abbreviated maledom. The term servant has also been used to refer to one devoted to the service of a lady.

Righty ho.

The next page took me to a site which claimed that up to ten percent of people enjoyed BDSM practices. *Really?* Seemed a high proportion to me. The nearest I'd come to a sexual peccadillo was adultery from the Scumbag and rubber gloves from Luciano. Then again, who was I to judge?

Maybe Hugh is my One-In-Ten?

The next page contained a description of some historic criminal cases brought against some sadomasochists who'd been a bit too enthusiastic in applying their punishments to each other.

Well, I'd better learn how to do it properly. I don't want to end up in court.

A vision of me beating the Scumbag back in my dream flashed in front my eyes and made me smile.

Am I developing my cruel side? Could I be a BDSM Mistress administering punishment to a willing submissive like Hugh?

I opened the next website, which took me straight to a dating site for the BDSM community. It was quite interesting to see that there were many more men who were submissive than women.

Is being a submissive more common for men? What do they get out of being beaten or humiliated?

I closed the computer. I decided that having one submissive in my life was more than enough for now.

* * * *

Wednesday evening was occupied with Andy and I taking our Uzbekistani agent to dinner. I was able to practice my

Russian for a while, but Andy felt a bit left out by this, so soon we all reverted to English to discuss business opportunities.

The agent was a charming ethnic Uzbek fluent in Uzbek, Russian, English, and French. He invited us to come and see him in Tashkent, and we enthusiastically agreed. Of course, there had to be a case to be presented to the boss to make him agree to pay the trip's expenses, but if the Uzbekistani agent sent us some students as promised, the boss might well see the business sense of our jolly boondoggle.

On Thursday evening back home, I continued my research. This time I Googled Marquis de Sade and spent the whole evening reading about his life, his books, and the eighteenth-century libertinism in France. I really enjoyed this. It was quite enlightening to learn how people lived and behaved in the past. I made a mental note to order one of his books online and read about his philosophy of how *no good deed goes unpunished*.

Friday arrived, the day of my lesson with Mistress Ulrika. Just before lunch I told Andy that I had a meeting in town and might be a bit late coming back in the afternoon. I might not even come back to work, and he would have to cover for me if necessary.

"Shag with Luciano, is it?" said Andy in a faux-Welsh accent, winking excessively and grinning.

"None of your damn business, boyo," I snapped back but couldn't help blushing as I said this.

"Thought so!" exclaimed Andy. "I'm never wrong about sex, you know, especially where it involves sex with well-hung men."

I picked up my coat and handbag and left. I got on the Tube and made the short journey required to get to Ulrika's place. I felt excited. I was entering the new world of BDSM. I was keen to learn more and find out as much as I could. I was joining the special ten percent of society who knew about the BDSM practices. Including my lovely Hugh.

* * * *

The address Mistress Ulrika had given me was in Central London near Hyde Park. One of those huge Georgian buildings, in the lower ground floor. In effect, it was the basement. *What an appropriate place for this sort of business.*

There was a video camera at the entrance, and as soon as I pressed the button to the side of the door, Mistress Ulrika let me in. The lounge looked like any other London flat in that area and had no signs or indication about the purpose of the activities inside.

Ulrika came towards me to greet me, and we shook hands. She was in her early thirties, probably about my age, good-looking with long dark hair. She was dressed very normally, in jeans and a t-shirt. Her hands were well-manicured with elegant, bright-red painted nails. Her handshake was firm.

"Welcome, Kate!" she said. "Now, the client will be here in about one hour, so we have time for the theory and signing the confidentiality agreement."

Her voice and appearance put me firmly in mind of the female judge who had passed sentence on the Scumbag in my dream. I shook this thought out of my head and focussed on the matter at hand.

I looked at her and asked, "What about the Dominatrix costume? Do I *really* need one? And if it's necessary for the learning process, do you have one which would fit me? And what do you mean by *the theory*? I didn't think this would be so complicated. What sort of theory is involved?"

"Well," Ulrika said. "First I would need to know what sort of things and activities your man enjoys. You know, here we can perform all sorts of services like bondage, knife play, cutting, piercing, and stuff like that. All of them have a risk of scarring or permanent injury. You need to be aware of this and learn how to perform it safely.

"It may take several lessons, and we would need to find a client who likes similar things like your partner, so you can practice under my supervision. So you would need to learn the theory first and then see in practice how it should be done."

Oh, dear God. What the fuck is all of this? Why does this need to be so complicated? I thought this was just about tying a person up and hitting him. I want to keep it light and loving for Hugh. I don't want to assault him with a deadly weapon!

"The riskiest is bondage," continued my teacher-to-be, "and you have to be very careful if your man is a bondage addict. You can cause him permanent injury from nerve damage. You'll be putting knots on his private parts, and if they're digging in, you can cut off circulation. You would need to monitor the temperature and the colour of the skin, and if his hands start to get tingly it can indicate loss of blood flow. You have to check in with him constantly and be like, *How are you feeling? Is this good? Do you have any tingling in your hands or other parts of your body?*"

"Oh," I said. "My man is definitely not into bondage or any sort of cutting or piercing. I think he just wants to be dominated and spanked a bit and he also mentioned a foot fetish."

I wasn't at all aware about Hugh's expectations, but one thing was for sure, if he wanted any of that shit like cutting him or tying up knots on his willy, I was going to run the proverbial mile. I added the foot fetish without being sure if he really liked it. I just wanted to sound more knowledgeable than I really was.

"Well," said Ulrika crisply, "in this case, you've got the lighter version of the submissive, not much work involved and a foot massage thrown in! I quite enjoy those with foot fetishes. Well, stomping hard on a client's bollocks is not my cup of tea," she continued, colourfully and rather gratuitously, "but if they desire it, I need to perform it. I try to be gentle with it, though, just in case they still want to produce some children with their wives." She laughed with a deep, cheerful voice.

"Ulrika," I said, "what made you decide to become a prosti... I mean, a Dominatrix?"

She seemed not to notice my near slip-of-the-tongue.

"Oh, this is just work, you know, hours to suit me and very good money. My husband thinks it's hilarious that I make more money than him working as a teacher in a high school."

A teacher? Was her husband one of our teachers? Hopefully not, but I decided to keep shtum about my place of work, just in case. The less she knew about me, the better.

"He does not mind you working as a... Dominatrix?"

Right word used this time.

Ulrika seemed amused by my question.

"Of course he doesn't. Working as a Dominatrix has nothing to do with sex. Nobody can touch you. We're Mistresses—we should be unattainable. Remember, you are a Mistress to dominate him and administer punishment. We do not allow any kind of normal relationship with these clients, they never get to see our bodies, and we treat them as scum." She paused. "Even if, actually, they're perfectly decent men in real life who just have these... needs. And I provide the service they require. For money, yes, but it's no more prostitution than the doctor who checks them for enlarged prostate is a prostitute."

I hoped that the expression on my face didn't look too sceptical at this last observation from Ulrika.

"And why would anybody want to come and experience this? I mean, being beaten or pierced with knives or tied up?" I asked.

I was curious about the motivation of a man who would pay for such painful experiences.

"Well," said Ulrika, "BDSM for some people is a necessary and essential part of their life. When they're experiencing pain or any other intense physical sensations, there's a release of endorphins—the body's natural opiates—which work to anaesthetise pain and also cause a feeling of euphoria. The endorphins produce a similar effect on the body to many illegal drugs, without the negative side effects and complications of drugs, addiction and all."

Ah, some science around it at last! Good, this I can relate to.

"This is combined with adrenaline the body would release in such situations," continued the Mistress. "And for some guys it just brings on these really overwhelming, euphoric sensations. For some people, it's almost like a spiritual kind of feeling. Others tell me it's just this cathartic release type of feeling... it's a very uplifting experience for them."

Ulrika went over to the kettle and put it on. She continued to download her analysis of BDSM motivations while scooping Darjeeling leaves into a pink teapot.

"For some men," she said, "it could be a sexual thing—but BDSM and sex are not necessarily synonymous. Although some men require physical punishment to get an erection and be able to perform sexually. It takes all sorts."

The kettle finished boiling. Ulrika picked it up and poured the contents into the teapot.

"So," she said, "have you asked your man what sort of things he really likes? The range of BDSM behaviours is enormous. It took me a long time to get trained in all aspects of being a Dominatrix and obviously I need to know how to train you properly once you've learned more about him."

Well, there's another discovery. Ulrika is trained to be a Dominatrix, so where did she train? Are there any schools or colleges for this? It seemed to be a serious profession, like a doctor or a nurse. *I'm working in the education sector, but I never heard of a college doing BDSM training. Do they also give out formal qualifications? Certificate or diploma? Does this lead to a National Vocational Qualification?*

Ulrika interrupted my thoughts.

"I guess," she said, "that this is just the beginning of your relationship with this man and you are not sure yet what he really enjoys. Don't worry. You will learn more about him later and give me the specifics at your next visit."

She brought over a mug of milky tea for me. "Obviously," she said, as she placed it on the coaster on the table, "you never came across any of the many BDSM societies and clubs. You should find out if your man is a member."

She sat down and watched me sip the tea. "Many of these clubs," she said, "are really quite respectable. Sort of like the Rotary Club, but with fewer clothes and pain. Others, though, are shady. Important to know where your man gets his kicks."

Holly golly, there are even clubs and societies for the sadomasochists? How little did I know living in my own closed world? Suddenly I felt uneducated and stupid and decided not to ask any more questions on the subject.

Somehow Ulrika had guessed all the things I didn't want to disclose to her. Was she reading my mind? I know I was pretty naïve asking her all these questions, so probably this made her realise my understanding was fairly limited. Anyway, she was right, and I decided it was time to stop asking questions and learn the ropes from her.

Ulrika returned to business. "Can you please sign the agreement, and we will change and go into the dungeon."

Ulrika was in charge of this establishment, and I was the apprentice keen to learn.

The non-disclosure agreement was simple, and I signed it quickly.

Ulrika asked me to strip to my panties and bra and put on

a black vinyl suit.

"Kate," she said, "please tie up your hair and put this blonde wig on. This gentleman likes blondes."

She did the same with her hair and put another black vinyl suit on. She also passed me a pair of black high-heeled, knee-length boots. "Put them on," she commanded, "size six, I think it's your size."

It was. And the whole ensemble was uncannily like how I was dressed in my recent dream, whipping the Scumbag. *Spooky.*

"Now for some background," said Ulrika as she changed. "This client's wife is blonde, but she doesn't want to be a Mistress anymore. Anyway, they have three children, and she is probably preoccupied with them. No child should witness such things, anyway."

As I put the high-heeled boots on, she handed me a black mask covering only my eyes. Very pretty, actually, sort of like a Viennese ballroom mask.

I looked at her. She'd completed her change of wardrobe and had transformed herself, and now she was a blonde Mistress Ulrika, commanding fear and obedience from all her slaves.

"Oh," said Ulrika, "I need to give you a name for the client. Is Mistress Jessica okay with you?"

The newly named Mistress Jessica nodded back. I hoped the nod came across as arrogant and dominating.

I was transformed and transfixed by my new appearance. I was dressed in a body-hugging suit and had a blonde wig and a Viennese-style face mask. I was like a creature from another planet—but surely a very sexy one.

"Hurry up, Kate, I mean Jessica. You need to see the dungeon before he comes!"

Ulrika's voice tore me away from the wall mirror in which I was admiring myself.

* * * *

I entered the dungeon. While as clean and neat as the rest of the flat, the back room was not brightly lit or airy. The atmosphere was, by contrast, rather heavy and humid, and was decorated in a quite different manner from the other rooms. Over the window was a thick black blind, so that no external light could penetrate. The walls were covered with velvet-cushioned wallpaper, a deep purple in colour. There was a black leather sofa with all sorts of black whips and other objects lying on it. I tried to remember my most recent dream, in which I seemed to be an expert with such things. But the knowledge my dream-self had had was gone. So my real, wide-awake self was at a loss to explain these items.

But Ulrika will show me, she will show me, I am sure. I am here to learn.

The aroma of real leather filled the air, which was heated to a temperature suitable for an indoor swimming pool. A single sixty-watt violet bulb, unshaded, was the sole source of illumination. There were other items there, but apart from a dark-blue painted cupboard for storage, there was none of the other furniture that made up a normal bedroom. Instead, various types of equipment abounded, which some would describe as appropriate for torture.

Mistress Ulrika—*I need to call her Mistress now*—took me around the room.

"This is the Fetters Sling," she said calmly as if describing the parts of a car, "and these are the Spanking Bench and Stretch Rack. This is a Bondage Bench, and this is the Sweet Torment St Andrews Cross."

Well, fuck me sideways. There was much more than I expected to see. *Oh, sweet Jesus, how can anybody even go on it?* But I said nothing.

Ulrika continued saying the names of these dreadful items of voluntary torture. "Here you have the canes, floggers, and whips," she said, showing me an array of sticks and cat-o'-nine-tails.

"And what are these for?" I pointed at some strange-looking contraptions hanging from the ceiling.

"This is all for Electric and Manual Suspension. Some clients want to be suspended while tied up," she explained.

"These are nipple clamps, dildos, and butt plugs. Here we have some iron cuffs, iron collar, and iron chains. And, finally, here we have an iron head cage, leather and rubber hoods, leather arm bondage sack, and leather hogtie."

Knock. Me. Down. With. A. Feather.

Ulrika continued to brief me, always with the air of someone describing the utterly commonplace.

"Obviously," she said, "there are also some ropes and bandages for the Mummy Addicts."

"Mummy Addicts?" I said. "What are the Mummy Addicts"?

"Ah," said Ulrika, "a speciality of the House of Ulrika, I think. There are no other Dominatrices who have taken this speciality to the heights available here."

She spoke in the manner of a three-Michelin-starred chef describing his special sauce for lobster thermidor.

"There are men, Kate — well, usually men," Ulrika corrected herself, "who want to be bandaged like a mummy and left in a crypt. As we have no crypts here, I invented a somewhat revolutionary replacement. I bandage them completely, head to toe, with only the tiniest opening for minimum breathing. This gives rise to the required sensory deprivation. Then, I take them and zip them totally up in a sleeping bag with just a small opening for air."

Ulrika paused to flick dust off her vinyl costume.

"I have two clients who enjoy this," she said. "I charge extra for it. I hope to market it more widely."

But not on eBay. I nearly said it out loud but was held back from doing so by the thought that sarcasm and irony were probably out of place in this context.

Ulrika continued her tour.

"Oh," she said. "I nearly forgot, this cabinet holds all the lubricants needed for the dildos and butt plugs. Very important."

I looked at the cupboard and saw several tubs of well-known oils, gels, creams, and unguents, some of which I'd used myself, albeit not stored in the industrial quantities required for Ulrika's business.

In the same cupboard, I also noticed a bottle of very expensive perfume with a brand label on it.

I pointed the bottle out to Ulrika. "Are you keeping your perfumes in here, too?" I asked her.

"Oh no," she said. "I normally use a quite different one, much cheaper than this ludicrously priced item. This is for one particular client of mine. I need to take this perfume just before he comes and spray it in the air. You know, his wife uses this perfume. The idea is that when I'm flogging him from behind, he can imagine it is her doing it to him. I suppose that part of him wants to believe that he's not being unfaithful to her, coming here naked and indulging his need for humiliation and pain. I have to keep silent during this treatment, as he does not want my voice, as distinct from her voice, to break the fantasy."

Golly gosh.

"Almost a pity," I observed, "that his wife cannot carry out the whipping herself. Fantasy meets reality, perhaps."

Ulrika stared at me blankly. "No, not a pity at all," she said. "If the wife was prepared to whip his bare ass, as I do, it would mean less business for me."

Ulrika slammed the cupboard door shut. "I think this is all when it comes to the equipment," she said.

So the inventory listing was complete. Mistress Ulrika was really proud of her dungeon and the equipment in it.

I was overwhelmed. Yes, the dungeon was well-equipped, that was for sure.

Did my potential husband-to-be expect m*e* to be proficient in using all of this?

"Where can you buy such equipment anyway? Would he need all of it? Holy shit, what I am getting myself into?" I murmured, quietly and to myself.

The bell rang, and Ulrika went to the hall. She looked at the intercom screen and then turned to me.

"Oh, we have our client, Mistress Jessica," Ulrika said. "It's only a one-hour appointment, but you should get an idea of what to do with your man when it comes to it."

The client entered. He was in his early fifties. Everything about him was average. Around five-foot-seven-inches, brown eyes, thinning brown hair. I'd passed many men like him on the street every day, and I would never have thought before that any of them might be going to his Mistress for a *session* to be beaten and humiliated and paying good money for this.

But there you go. You learn something new every day.

As soon as he entered, Mistress Ulrika shouted at him in a voice which commanded immediate respect and obedience.

"You, you dirty dog, you are five minutes late. We've been waiting for you, wasting our valuable time. Mistress Jessica is with me today, and she's very annoyed with this. You deserve some extra punishment today. Double the punishment from two Mistresses."

He immediately entered into the spirit of the process and cowed at the well-deserved criticism.

"Yes, Mistress," he whimpered, bowing his head submissively. "I am sorry, I deserve extra punishment, please. Mistress Jessica, nice to meet you. I will love more punishment from you, too, please."

"Not now, you utter worm," said Mistress Ulrika with contempt. "You will need to wait. Do you imagine we are here to obey *you*? You've got a nerve. Now strip. Take off all of your clothes. We need to examine you."

The client undressed eagerly. Given our high heels, we now towered over him, a naked pink fat man with his head bowed. He had a pot belly, and his willy was shrunken and in a sorry state. He tried to cover it with his hand, but Ulrika screeched with apparent fury and hit his hand with the riding crop she suddenly seemed to be carrying.

"Who told you to cover your cock, such as it is, slave?" she yelled. "When I want you anything but totally naked, exposed and at my mercy, I'll tell you! Fucking take your hands off yourself *right now.*"

She grabbed him hard by the balls. He winced and moved back a bit.

"You think I like having to deal with pathetic scum like you, worm?" she hissed in his ear while holding tight to his balls. "You think I like having to punish you as you deserve?"

The man had gone the colour of puce and was standing on his toes as Ulrika pulled his testicles up.

"No, Mistress," he gasped. "I mean, yes, Mistress," he continued in the same tone. "I mean, I don't know, Mistress, whatever you want, Mistress."

Ulrika let go of his balls. Then she slapped him on the face. "You're lower than the whale-shit, aren't you, slave? Not much better than pondweed?"

I watched all this in complete astonishment. It was sort of a bit like sex, but not as I knew it. It felt like an out-of-body experience. It was quite bizarre and yet, quite real. I thought about my boss coming here for such a session and nearly laughed. Ulrika heard my suppressed giggle.

"You see, worm, Mistress Jessica is laughing at you, a pathetic excuse for a man—you deserve to be punished." And with these words, she whipped him on his bare bottom with the riding crop. Then the crop was applied to his thighs near his genitals.

He screamed out in pain.

"So was it hard enough?" she asked.

"Harder, Mistress, harder," yelled the naked man, who'd just been called worm, pondweed, whale-shit.

So he wants more pain, more humiliation?

"Now..." Mistress Ulrika was in commanding form, towering over the fellow. "You dirty dog, tell me the safe word. You know what the safe word means. It means that I will stop whatever I am doing because you cannot take it anymore."

This was obviously an important bit—health and safety regulation etcetera. Even if done within the confines of a session of physical abuse.

"Mistress, please hit me again, I can take more, give me more," shouted the man, bending over and gratuitously pulling his buttocks apart so that I got a good, if unwanted, view of his russet brown anal opening.

"The safe word!" Ulrika demanded while whipping him again.

I noticed red marks on his buttocks. This must have hurt, yet he seemed to enjoy it.

"Ice cream, ice cream," he said. "Mistress, the safe word is ice cream."

"That's right," Ulrika yelled back at him. "Everyone screams for ice cream!"

Now Ulrika moved away and seemed to calm herself. She stopped whipping him and put the riding crop on a chair nearby. She spoke more calmly in a quieter voice. "Now, dog, you deserve a prize. You are allowed to lick my boots, the left one first, then the right. Be sure to clean them well."

The client dropped on all fours, and Ulrika put her left foot forward, nearly kicking him in his face. He put his hands on the back of her heels and started licking her boots, making slurping noises as he did it.

"That's enough!" She violently withdrew her left foot and pushed her right foot forward, intentionally kicking him in his face.

"Now, you dirty dog, lick this one."

The man obeyed and occupied himself licking her right boot.

"That's good. You are a dog, a stinking, dirty dog. Now you lick Mistress Jessica's boots."

The client moved on all fours towards me, wiggling his bottom, just as if he were a real dog wagging his tail. He started licking my boots. I felt paralysed and couldn't move, staring with fascination at his quivering, naked body at my feet.

Is this what it takes to keep some men happy?

I had very mixed feelings. I felt bad for humiliating this nice man and had to remind myself that it was his desire to do this. What's more, he was paying for all of this treatment and enjoyed it.

Good grief, aren't men strange. Is Hugh into licking boots, too? Would I be able to respect him if he was?

Suddenly, Ulrika poked the man with the riding crop, forcing him to cease licking my boots. He looked up at her, his face full of whimpering bliss, awaiting instructions.

"And now, you disgusting scum," said Ulrika stonily, "your second prize today, put this head mask on."

"Yes, Mistress. Thank you, I love the mask."

Ulrika seemed to go red with fury at this last remark. She bent down and grabbed his balls again. "I don't care if you love the mask or not, you fucking tosser," she yelled. "I'm not here to do things you love, slave. You're here to do my bidding." She slapped him on the bum. "For that presumption, shithead, the mask will be worn in the tight position, so you feel *my* fury through *your* agony."

Despite all this, the client's face seemed to register joy,

almost ecstasy. He eagerly put the black leather head mask on, and Ulrika fastened it at the back. After finishing the fastening and tying the ends, she slapped him hard on the buttocks again for good measure. He seemed to quiver with delight in response.

The mask covered his entire head. Apart from the space for him to breathe through his nose, and an opening for a mouth, the mask was complete in its effect, preventing him from seeing and giving him only limited hearing.

Mistress Ulrika then skilfully tied up his wrists with leather straps. Then she attached them to metal rings, which in turn hung from the ceiling suspended on ropes. She went to the side wall and tugged on a cord. This caused the ring to go up, and the client was forced to stand on tiptoes by the shortness of the leather straps. Now Ulrika took two nipple clamps and clipped them to his nipples. He made some muffled noises.

Urr, that's gotta hurt. I wouldn't want anything like those clipped to my delicate areas.

Ulrika must have sensed my uneasiness at her actions and whispered in my ear, "That's how he likes it. If he didn't, he'd yell the safe word, and it would stop. Now you have to whip him several times on his buttocks. Don't go over the top. He can't have any skin damage — his wife would not be happy finding out about his visits here."

She put a black whip in my hand and directed me towards the man's behind.

I wanted to protest, saying I was here to learn and not to beat up this poor man myself. Then I realised that this was all part of the learning, this was the practical part of being a Mistress. *Do I have it within me to do this?* Well, I needed to check, I wasn't going to give up without trying...

So I closed my eyes and hit the client on his buttocks with the whip. I opened my eyes and noticed that he didn't move in response, and there was no sound coming from his mouth.

He could have had a heart attack – shall I stop now? Will I be prosecuted if I caused him a heart attack? Is Ulrika insured against such prosecution?

Ulrika clearly noticed my hesitation and told me, "He is okay, don't worry. Hit him another time, don't hesitate. Do it now."

So I hit him again on his buttocks, keeping my eyes fully open this time. Again, no reaction from the man.

I supposed I was just far too gentle with him.

Ulrika had obviously realised this and ordered me in a stern, loud voice, "Harder, you need to hit that pathetic wanker harder, Mistress Jessica. He deserves a great punishment for keeping you waiting."

She walked up to me, took the cat-o'-nine-tails from me, and hit the client hard on his back. He moaned softly in response.

Ulrika gave me the whip back and seemed to mouth the words "Give it some welly!" at me. So, encouraged by his response and seeing that he was still alive and responding, I hit the poor man harder, and he moaned again.

I supposed I'd had the desired effect on him, but my heart wasn't really in it. I knew it was all play-acting, I knew he wanted this treatment, but in front of my eyes, I saw a picture of his wife and three young children waiting for him at home. The wife waiting for him with dinner already cooked and the children waiting for Daddy to come home and play with them.

I knew it was only lunch hour, so why was my mind bringing his family into it?

What's wrong with me? Why do I get such pictures in my mind of a family waiting for their husband and father? Am I mad?

Anyway, shouldn't he be spending his money on them, rather than paying Mistress Ulrika?

This was the practical part of me justifying my mixed feelings towards the client.

The client moaned louder, and I thought that I'd hit him too hard. I stopped and looked at Ulrika.

"That was the right strength," she hissed. "Come on. This is how he likes it. You are getting there!" She waved her arms encouragingly.

I suppressed my conscience and hit the man again.

He moaned something which sounded like, "Thank you, Mistress Jessica. Thank you so much."

Now Ulrika came over to the client, and I saw that she was holding a dildo in one hand, putting lube on it with the other.

"It's a butt plug—it has to be big to fit into this scumbag's fat, sweaty, dirty butt-hole," she explained loudly, partly for my edification, and partly for his humiliation, all the while expertly inserting the well-lubricated dildo into his anus and switching the vibration on.

He moaned in response to the effects he was experiencing from the lubricated, vibrating, penis-shaped, ten-inch plastic dildo, of which five inches had disappeared into his body. The moan was ecstatic, and his buttocks—as fat and sweaty as Ulrika had described them—quivered in response to the vibration.

His own, previously placid, much shorter and thinner penis was now erect and looking towards the ceiling.

"I can assure you," whispered Ulrika, seeing that I had noticed the erection, "that this is as hard as this gentleman has ever got it, certainly far more erect than it ever is in more ordinary sexual circumstances."

Bugger me, if this is what he needs to get an erection, my knowledge to date about male sexuality is lacking a lot.

"Well, now, we can leave him to it. Time for a cup of tea for us," Ulrika said, exiting the room and closing the dungeon's door behind us. "I'm thirsty after all that yelling. Come to the kitchen."

* * * *

"How do you find it so far?" she asked while putting the kettle on.

"I-I find it interesting," I said, a bit hesitantly. It was all I could muster.

"Would you prefer coffee?" Ulrika took a bottle of milk out of a small fridge in the corner.

"Yes, please, black and strong." I needed something stronger than tea but obviously alcohol was not on offer — we were still working, this was just a tea break.

"Why do they want the mask on?" The unexpected eagerness of the client to put the mask on was still puzzling me.

"Well," said Ulrika, sipping her tea, "the mask gives him sensory deprivation. He can't see or hear much, and this highlights his pain and the pleasure he gets from it. I have one client who even puts on the iron mask, and believe me, that one is heavy."

She put the coffee in front of me, and I added two spoons of sugar to it — no time to think about empty calories, I needed something strong. *Next time I will bring a flask of whisky with me.* Irish coffee would do me good now. *Not sure, though, that I really want a next time...*

"Your husband, does he come here? I mean, to this dungeon? Does he like to be a submissive?" I asked. It was obvious that this one-bedroom flat was rented out only for these sorts of services and was not lived in.

Ulrika laughed. It was the giggly laughter of a happy little girl. Such a contrast with her persona in the dungeon.

"Oh no," she replied, "not at all. We have a very conventional sex life. He would never allow me to treat him in such a way. No, my Dominatrix stuff is only with the work here. The earnings are good, and I can arrange my times around my family life and my university study."

I was intrigued by that last comment.

"Are you studying at university, Ulrika? Is the university degree in domination? Master of Arts in Dominancy and Whipping or anything like that?"

Ulrika laughed again, even more loudly. "Oh no, Kate, not at all. What a delightful idea, though. I am studying to be a lawyer. I'll be finishing my Masters soon. I already have a Bachelor degree." She gulped at her milky tea. "My dream is to become a criminal barrister."

"Wow," I said, "a criminal barrister with a great understanding of all BDSM matters. You'll be the only one in the country with such knowledge. Could be useful, defending people."

I was impressed with Ulrika's determination to become a criminal barrister. She was a lady of similar kind to me. She was just working, trying to make some money and delivering the service her clients desired.

A good woman, fighting to make her way in the world, while doing no harm and possibly doing some good.

"Ulrika," I said, "what happens after you qualify? Will you carry on with all this, sort of part-time, once you're a fully flogged barrister... I mean, a fully *fledged* barrister."

We laughed at my little slip of the tongue.

"Oh, I think so," she said, "at least until I'm really coining it at the Bar. A criminal junior makes very small beer money, you know. I bet you I'll need to keep going with all this for some time."

We finished our drinks, and Ulrika looked into her appointments book lying on the table.

"Well," she said, "our next appointment will be here in thirty minutes. I always have little breaks between clients' appointments, just in case they bump into and recognise each other. That would cause some embarrassment, although some men do like to share their sessions with other clients. I like it, too, as I get to make double, or even triple, money."

"Who are the men who come here?" I asked. "Is there any specific type of a man who... hmm... requires your services?" I was very curious to know as much as possible about this new avenue of sexual gratification. Things I'd never experienced and had only a vague idea they even existed.

Until now.

"Oh," said Ulrika, "you would be surprised. The men come from all walks of life, but now thinking about it, I have many more high-powered clients than those in low-paid jobs."

"Is this about the money they pay you? Those in low-paid jobs can't afford it?"

"No, definitely not, we are reasonable with our charges." She seemed almost offended, but only for a moment. She then considered the question carefully. "You know, Kate, I think it's more that those men who are in top jobs, in positions of power, they come here to be treated like shit to relieve the stress of their jobs. I have plenty of barristers, bankers, and judges as my clients." She laughed. "Maybe one of my QC clients will give me pupillage in his chambers in return for free bondage in my chambers!"

She examined her appointments book. She smiled and looked up at me.

"Now my next client," she said, "is one of the high-powered clan. He is the one who likes the iron mask. Well, he's into everything — you name it, bondage, cutting, electrocuting, such an eclectic taste. He is my best client and leaves great tips. So would you like to stay for another session, Kate? You would learn much more while we work on him. He booked a double appointment today for two hours. No extra charges for you if you want to learn more."

I felt flattered. My new friend, the trainee barrister and Mistress of Domination, obviously liked my company and wanted me to learn more.

But I felt a bit full of it all for now. I needed to get out and take stock.

"Maybe next time," I said. "I should be getting back to work."

This was a blatant lie as I'd taken the afternoon off and told Andy to cover for me. Officially I was checking students' accommodation.

Then I thought about Ulrika's offer again. I was somehow fascinated by all this.

I wouldn't mind spending another hour asking her questions about the men who come here.

This would allow me to learn more and would explain Hugh's needs and desires, but I was not sure I had the energy to whip more naked buttocks or plug their bottoms with dildos.

I might do a tiny bit of butt whipping on Hugh, but this was as far as I was prepared to go.

I cannot kiss a man who licks my shoes. Not very hygienic, is it?

I thought that foot fetishes were about massaging my feet, not licking my boots!

"Come with me now," said Ulrika. "The client's session is nearly finished."

We went back into the darkened room, and Ulrika untied the client's wrists, removed the dildo from his bottom, and unfastened the head mask.

He took it off his head, and I saw his face completely changed. All the frowns had gone, and he seemed very relaxed. He was a different man and seemed at least ten years younger. When he'd first come here, it had looked as if he was carrying the whole world on his shoulders. Now he appeared different, his whole body somehow rejuvenated and more vigorous. He was transformed into another person, much nicer to see and be with.

He was cheerful and happy, full of joy with a big smile on his face.

"Oh, thank you, Mistresses, that was wonderful. Can I have both of you at my next session, please? I'll pay double if necessary," he added quickly.

He dressed and withdrew from his jacket's inside pocket a wad of cash and gave it to Ulrika.

"Can I book the same time next week with you, Mistress Ulrika, and I hope Mistress Jessica will be here, too? I quite liked having two Mistresses attending to my needs. This was the best session I've ever had. Thank you very much."

"Well, we haven't decided yet. Mistress Jessica is in training. Now go and be a good boy." Ulrika opened the door for him.

He left, and I decided to go, too, but Ulrika wanted to have a chat.

"You know, Kate, you are a natural for this type of work. You look great in the costume, the clients would love you, and I could do with someone helping me from time to time. What would you say to this? Listen," she continued before I could answer, "the next appointment is actually my best client, as I said before. He comes here nearly every day. I could train you on him. He is into everything, so you would learn quickly — you do not have be emotionally involved in all of this. It might seem overwhelming at first, but you will quickly learn to be detached, and this is a good source of income. You could treat it as a part-time job on top of your regular one. Few hours a week, something different to do."

She continued her pitch. "I'm sure your man will appreciate your skills, once you're fully trained. It may even strengthen your relationship if he knows you are accepting his peccadilloes. So what do you say, Kate?" Ulrika was waiting patiently for my answer.

"Well, Ulrika," I said, "I'm really not sure, I am quite busy at work."

She was visibly disappointed with my answer, and I felt bad. Ulrika was such a nice person, and I really liked her.

"Okay," I said hastily, trying to erase Ulrika's disappointment at my previous answer. "I promise I will think about it and let you know soon. I promise."

Ulrika's face immediately lit up, and I felt better for it.

I needed time to think about this Dominatrix business. All of this was new to me, and I really wasn't sure about my own emotions yet.

I'd already taken the boots and the black vinyl suit off and changed into my own clothes. Oh, I needed to take the wig off, too, even though I quite fancied myself as a bleached platinum blonde. I might need to change my colour the next time I saw my posh hairdresser.

"Kate, I know you're not used to it, but believe me, you can learn quite quickly, and you will find it rewarding. You are highly intelligent, and you will learn this is a role-play, nothing to get hung up about. It is also good money," Ulrika persevered, not prepared to give up on me and encouraged by my promise to think about it.

Before I could say anything to her endorsement of me as a future Dominatrix, the doorbell rang, and I could vaguely see with the corner of my eye the face of another eager man on the screen, presumably the next client.

Ulrika answered the bell ring with a stern voice, her Dominatrix persona back in full swing. "You are fucking fifteen minutes early, you piece of shit. What did I say about early fucking calls? No way will I let you in. You need to go and come back in fifteen minutes' time, not a minute earlier. Do not be late, either, just bang on time."

I could hear his reply through the intercom.

"I am sorry, Mistress, I am very sorry. I'll go now and come back in exactly fifteen minutes. I really need a good session today, too much stress at work. I know the rules, but I was too keen to see you. I didn't notice the time, I apologise."

His voice, although distorted by the speaker, sounded oddly familiar, but I couldn't place it.

Who is he? Do I know him?

I came near the screen and saw the eager face of Mistress Ulrika's next client properly.

I was shocked. I knew him all right.

This was the same man I'd had a date with a week ago and another one planned for tomorrow.

It was my Hugh.

Bloody hell! He is her best client! I said nothing—I was speechless anyway and would not have been able to say anything even if I'd tried.

"Mistress, now I'll go, and I'll come back in the next fifteen minutes as ordered."

"Fourteen minutes now," shouted Ulrika.

"Yes, Mistress, fourteen minutes, thank you for correcting me."

His face disappeared from the screen.

I was still shocked but kept a straight face.

Could I admit to Ulrika that she was servicing my potential boyfriend—would-be-husband? How would she react? Would she tell him about my visit here and the purpose of it?

Would this change anything if he knew that I know?

I decided that there was no need for any of this. But I had an overwhelming urge to get out of this establishment urgently.

"Thank you, Ulrika, for your lesson. This was very, very enlightening." I'd found the right word to use. "I'll be in touch, promise." I was babbling away, trying to escape. Yes, after seeing Hugh's face I felt I needed to escape out into the open air.

I kissed her on both cheeks. She kissed me in return and

hugged me tightly.

"Listen, Kate," she said. "If you need any more lessons or even if you would like to meet up for a chat, do let me know, and please remember you can always have a job here."

She put something in my coat pocket as I was leaving.

* * * *

I walked up the stairs from the basement to street level and took a deep breath of the fresh winter air. I saw Hugh's Bugatti, parked in the street around two hundred yards away.

Has he seen me? Probably not, he would not expect me here. Shall I go towards him and tell him that I know about his sessions with Mistress Ulrika? How would he react? Probably with anger – this would definitely kill the possibility of our relationship, that's for sure.

But he's not doing anything illegal, anyway. What gives me the right to barge into his life in that way?

What about my hopes for a relationship and a family with him?

I really wanted to understand, to find a way to accept his peculiar needs, to not see it as potential sexual infidelity but a sort of stress-relieving hobby.

Other men play squash for hours, what's so different about this? I tried to persuade myself.

I wanted to learn about his specific needs, and that's why I went to visit Ulrika and learn from her. I remembered our lovely session in his car and his kisses on my hand and on my lips. *He's definitely capable of normal sex, I'm sure.*

I put my hat down and walked quickly in the opposite direction. Tears were streaming down my face. What I was crying for? I was not sure...

It wasn't the place or the session with the client – it was seeing Hugh's face in the monitor and realising that it was my man who was Ulrika's best client going there nearly every day. To be whipped, cut, and electrocuted. For pleasure.

I wanted to run away, to be as far as possible from here. I needed to put a lot of distance between me and Ulrika's establishment, and Hugh waiting patiently in the car to be allowed to lick Ulrika's boots or worse.

What could be worse? Putting the iron mask on and looking like an alien. Would he expect me to perform such service on him? Does he have an iron mask at home and a collection of whips, too?

Would he still visit Ulrika if he had a family with me?

I saw myself in my imagination some years into the future, sitting at home with two young children on my lap looking at the clock and waiting for my husband, who I knew was not working late on the trading floor, but was stripped naked and screaming with pleasure while enjoying Mistress Ulrika's services.

Would I be I strong enough to put up with this? Would I be loving enough to forgive him? His previous wife obviously was not. Was I a better woman than her?

My head was full of questions I couldn't answer. I needed a chat with a friend about all of this.

What friend? None of my girlfriends are into this stuff. As far as I know, anyway. Who shall I talk to?

Hugh himself, perhaps, after he'd finished today's two-hour session? I shuddered at the very idea of such a conversation. I wanted to talk about him and about the possible life I could have with him. He was the problem to be solved—I could scarcely discuss him with him!

And what about the date tomorrow? Should I go ahead with it or cancel it?

But I quite fancy a dinner in the Ritz, said some silly voice in my head.

Well, let's get you one then... This was another part of me, the sane one.

* * * *

So I called the Ritz and made a dinner reservation for two for that night. Then I called Andy, who was still in the office.

"Hi, Andy," I said. "How do you fancy dinner tonight in the Ritz? With absolutely no risk of having to have sex with your companion afterwards."

"The Ritz?" Andy was impressed. "I would love to, but it is expensive, I believe. You need to be as rich as Cresus or have the golden touch of King Midas to afford it."

"Well, now you can afford it, seven tonight, my treat."

"Perfect," said my gay assistant. "Nice and early. I'm meeting my new man, Vinny, for a little bit of how's-your-father at eleven, so thanks to you, my beautiful and surprisingly suddenly wealthy boss, I will be well-fed ahead of what promises to be an explosive encounter in Vinny's shower."

"Outstanding," I said. "I'll see you at seven. And, Andy, please put your jacket and tie on. Otherwise you will not be allowed in."

I got home following the usual crush on the Central Line.

Time to have a shower to wash off the experience of the last few hours.

I took my coat off and checked the pocket where Ulrika had put something. It was a wad of cash. Exactly the same amount as I'd paid her for the lesson.

Was I getting a refund because the grateful client had coughed up extra in return for being humiliated by two Mistresses, instead of the usual one? Or was I being paid to get me to agree to become her Dominatrix companion, her apprentice? Or did she just return my money because she liked me?

I guess I'll never know now. I'm not going to continue my lessons with her anymore.

The shock of seeing Hugh's face on the screen and knowing that he had sessions with her had put me off from getting any more *education* in that whole area.

At seven sharp, I got to the Ritz, where Andy was already waiting for me at the bar, sipping a ridiculously expensive, but perfectly concocted, chilled vodka martini. He was dressed to kill, with a sort of understated cool that would drive women wild with frustration.

Good thing I know to expect only a girlfriend experience from Andy.

He stood to greet me, pointing to the glass of single malt whisky that was waiting for me, and which he'd ordered on my account. I looked around and noticed that all the women in the bar were ogling Andy. *Half the men, too.*

Once we were at our table consuming hors d'oeuvres with alacrity — only now did I realise how hungry I was — and while waiting for our starters, I filled Andy in on all the details of today's events. I didn't omit the specifics of the surprise arrival at Ulrika's dungeon of my new *possible partner for life and husband*, neither Ulrika's description of him as her number one client nor her report of his addiction to extreme pain at her hands.

"You know, Andy," I said, a little indistinctly through my half-chewed fourth vol-au-vent, "I could live with it. He seems a good man, but if he thinks I'm not as good a Dominatrix as Ulrika, he'll still go and visit her. I'd just have to put up with it, particularly if I'm getting satisfaction from him in a more... err... conventional fashion. After all, what he's doing is not illegal, and he's not seeing a prostitute. As you pointed out the other day, BDSM isn't about sex. I think I should see it as similar to one's man going off to play football or squash, just a form of exercise, done away from me, and extraneous to our relationship."

Andy checked his watch. Again.

I scowled. "Andy," I said. "It's only eight o'clock. You've still got three hours before Vinicius takes you to his shower for your first ride over the jumps. I'd be grateful if you would pay attention and give me the benefit of your advice.

This ain't a free lunch, you know."

I got back to the current conundrum of my own love life. "You see, Andy, I'm sure that Hugh does straight sex, too, and I've no doubt he can satisfy a woman more normally. He can keep this Dominatrix stuff separate. I don't think it's something I really want to be involved in myself."

Andy didn't speak, he just stuffed his face with hors d'oeuvres, but I could tell from his eyes that he was, at last, paying attention and thinking hard about my problem.

"But," I continued, "if I don't do the domination thing on him, whipping, cutting, all the horrible things that Ulrika does so professionally, so dispassionately, he'll just develop a secret life in BDSM away from me, and I couldn't bear that. So somehow, I'll have to become like Ulrika, the Mistress of a dungeon, in which I can pleasure my man by torturing him."

I shuddered. "I don't know what to do, Andy. Should I develop a relationship with Hugh, inclusive of me becoming his Mistress Jessica, or should I just let him deal with Ulrika for that side of his sexual needs? And just pretend it's no more important than him going to the sports club for a game of squash?"

Andy leaned back. As he did so, the back of his chair bumped into a uniformed waiter carrying our main course — two plates of pied de cochon garnished with potatoes dauphinoise and spinach. The waiter — a darkly handsome, early twenty-something with an air of youthful innocence — brilliantly saved the dishes from crashing to the floor. Andy was full of apologies and concern for the waiter, even after he'd successfully laid the plates down on our table.

As the waiter left, Andy whispered something in his ear. The waiter blushed and nodded, shyly but vehemently.

"What was that all about?" I said, grinning. "As if I didn't know."

"Well," said Andy. "Given my negligence in leaning my chair into that beautiful boy and causing him such distress, I've offered him a drink. At my flat. Tomorrow night. Sans waiter's uniform, naturally. Sans everything, I'm hoping."

He called over the sommelier to fill our wine glasses.

"Good grief, Andy," I said after the sommelier had stepped back, "tonight it's Vinny, tomorrow the young waiter. And what happened to those two other men you were seeing?"

"Eduardo and Tristram? I'm still seeing them," said Andy, "separately, of course. I maintain a sort of unstated fiction that I'm faithful to each, as they do with me. All of us are lying, but since nothing is ever actually said either way, frankly it works. Plenty of sexual variety and everyone is happy."

"Well perhaps then we can return to my little problem. Honestly, Andy, what do I do? Go with Hugh and be his Mistress Jessica, or go with Hugh and let him get his other kicks with Ulrika?"

Andy sighed. He dabbed his mouth delicately with his laundered napkin, leaned across the table, and took my hand in his. "Kate," he said. "I know you're still hurting after what that bastard from the Customs did to you, and I'm sure that, in your mind's eye, you visualise happy-ever-after with this Hugh guy, but I'm worried that you're selling yourself short in reaction to how that Paul treated you. You don't have to live with second best. You are a truly fantastic, beautiful woman who deserves the best man there could possibly be."

He stopped and sat back.

"Now," he said. "Doubtless in most ways I can see how this Hugh fits the bill. Rich, young—ish—handsome, good personality. But this domination thing is serious. It's not a case of just a bit of light bum spanking now and again. He's hardcore.

"And that would seriously get in the way of you developing a good relationship with him over the long-term if you're not also heavily into it. And by the sound of your reaction to the session with Ulrika, you're not going to be able to develop a taste for whipping the man you love into a coma or cutting him until he bleeds.

"And how would that fit with family life? You gonna leave the kids with a nanny while you and Hugh pop off to the dungeon for a little torture time? I don't think so, Kate. I just can't see you doing it. More to the point, nor can you.

"His first wife obviously couldn't take all this, either, and ended up with the local builder. Do you fancy ending up seeking solace in the arms of a tradesman, while your lovely husband is with his Mistress, getting beaten black and blue?"

He stopped his peroration to allow the entry into his mouth of a substantial forkful of pied de cochon. When he'd completed its mastication, a look of bliss on his face as he chewed, he returned to the theme. "And worst of all, Kate, Hugh has lied to you. He's told you he's only into a little of the light stuff, when really he's Ulrika's best client, into the heaviest and most dangerous BDSM there is. Not a great start to the relationship, is it, girl?"

A mouthful of the dauphinoise followed. And then Andy delivered the coup de grace.

"Dump him, Kate," he said. "Just dump him. There are plenty of good, straight men out there. Find the one you deserve. Don't put up with this sort of shit."

He looked at his watch again. I looked at mine, too. It was half past nine.

"So," continued my adviser, "you were supposed to have dinner with him here tomorrow. Are you still going to?"

Andy became distracted once again by the reappearance

of the beautiful young waiter. This allowed me the few moments of silence I needed to make my decision, taking account of all that Andy had said.

"No, not anymore," I said when Andy's eyes had finally abandoned their fixation with the waiter's pert bottom. "You've convinced me, Andy. I'll make some excuse and get out of it. I don't want to progress the relationship with Hugh. I deserve better than this, even if he does seem perfect in so many other ways."

I sighed, my decision tinged with regret. "Anyway..." I toyed with the wineglass and stared into it in the hope the answer to all my life difficulties would be found in it. "It would be difficult for me to keep secret my knowledge of his visits to Mistress Ulrika. I don't know how he would react once he found out that I know about them. I think the relationship just wouldn't develop into something meaningful, anyway."

"That's great, Kate, well done. This is the right decision. You deserve the best. And he's out there for you. But it's not this guy. Just as I've said." Andy seemed very pleased with himself. Then, "I've got an idea," he suddenly said. He leaned forward. "What's Hugh's surname?"

I didn't quite follow why this was relevant to anything. "Cartwright," I said, showing him Hugh's business card. "Why?"

"I'm going to the reception to cancel his booking for tomorrow. I'll tell them that I'm Mr Cartwright and we're having our dinner tonight instead."

I tried to protest, but he'd already left his chair.

"All done." He came back, still laughing. "I love pranks like that, and it'll serve him right."

"Really, Andy," I said primly, "that was very immature, you know. Still, I suppose I should be grateful you didn't try to get off with the receptionist while you were cancelling

Hugh's booking."

"I can explain that," said Andy, still very pleased with his evening's work. "She was a woman."

I laughed. "Well, yes, I can see how her gender would raise insurmountable obstacles for you in that regard. And I'm really grateful for your advice, Andy. You're a great pal to have. There's no one else with whom I could possibly discuss this kind of thing."

I raised my glass of wine. "Here's to me finding the Real Mister Right. And here's to you having several orgasms tonight with Vinny."

Andy raised his glass, too. "Great stuff, Kate. And thanks for dinner. Onwards and upwards!"

Will the story finish here? Will Kate leave Hugh because of his peccadilloes, or will she stay with him and try to change him? More to come about this in the next book about Kate the Apprentice Dominatrix.

ABOUT THE AUTHOR

D.V. Roberts lives in the beautiful county of Kent in South-East England, with her husband, children, cats, dogs and chickens. She has pursued many careers in different parts of Europe and Russia, from engineering to education and from the medical sector to catering. Kate's "Adventures" are but echoes of Roberts' own journey through life and men, to achieve her own Happy Ever After.

www.ingramcontent.com/pod-product-compliance
Lightning Source LLC
Chambersburg PA
CBHW070523130626
46555CB00003B/1319